D1572577

The Cowboy's Counterfeit Fiancée

Cowboys of Whistle Rock Ranch, Book Six

Contemporary Western Romance

SHIRLEEN DAVIES

Books Series by Shirleen Davies

<u>Historical Western Romances</u>

Redemption Mountain

MacLarens of Fire Mountain Historical

MacLarens of Boundary Mountain

<u>Romantic Suspense</u>

Eternal Brethren Military Romantic Suspense

Peregrine Bay Romantic Suspense

<u>Contemporary Western Romance</u>

Cowboys of Whistle Rock Ranch

MacLarens of Fire Mountain Contemporary

Macklins of Whiskey Bend

Find all my books at: **https://shirleendavies.com/ books/**

The best way to stay in touch is to subscribe to my newsletter. Go to my Website ***www.shirleendavies.com*** and fill in your email and name in the Join My Newsletter boxes. That's it!

The best way to stay in touch is to subscribe to my newsletter. Go to my Website ***www.shirleendavies.com*** and fill in your email and name in the Join My Newsletter boxes. That's it!

Description

He agreed to be her fake fiancée.
What happens when fake no longer applies?

Logan Sawyer has a lot to learn. His new job, working with his older stepbrother, keeps him busy, as does his developing friendship with a female ranch hand at a neighboring ranch. Both present challenges. The first because he has almost no ranch experience. The second because he can count the number of friends he's ever had on one hand.

Samantha Miller is one of the best workers on Whistle Rock Ranch. Her level of experience has been gained through long days doing jobs most women would shun. She has little time for anything else. Except her growing friendship with the younger, much less experienced, hand at the neighboring ranch.

Working hard during the week, the two friends enjoy each other's company, spending Saturday nights in town, eating dinner and dancing to a local band. Theirs is an easy camaraderie, talking and laughing with no expectations. The same as any friendship.

Until a ghost from Sam's past shows up, threatening the life she's built at Whisper Lake. The surprise arrival also coincides with menacing events at the ranch and in town.

Unprepared to confront the danger, Sam and Logan devise a plan to protect themselves and their budding friendship. A plan which includes tricking those closest to them.

But will it be enough?

The Cowboy's Counterfeit Fiancée, book six in the Cowboys of Whistle Rock Ranch Contemporary Western Romance series, is a clean and wholesome, full-length novel with an HEA.

The Cowboy's Counterfeit Fiancée

Chapter One

Whistle Rock Ranch
July

The steer broke the rope, powering itself into the arena. Panicking, it ran from Wyatt Bonner's position on the animal's left side as the rope settled over the steer's head. Seconds later, Virgil Redstar approached from the right. Swinging the rope in the air, he let it go. The crowd whooped when the rope caught one of the steer's hind feet.

Logan Sawyer cheered with the rest of the dude ranch guests as Wyatt and Virgil continued to demonstrate team roping during the weekly ranch rodeo. Both had competed in high school and college in the same event, as well as participating in saddle bronc riding. Guests at the ranch loved their demonstrations.

Logan worked at an adjoining ranch where his older brother, Quinn Sawyer, was the foreman. A few of their ranch hands participated in the demonstrations. They weren't paid for their efforts, but the payoff came from the heart-pounding adrenaline rush of the challenge.

"Hey, Logan. Are you going to compete?" Samantha Miller, a Whistle Rock ranch hand, stood next to him, her gaze on Wyatt and Virgil.

"Not a chance, Sam. Did I hear you're going to ride the

barrels?"

"Nah. I've never done barrel racing. I hear Virgil has a gal from another ranch driving over. She should be here any minute." She glanced over her shoulder at the sound of a vehicle entering the parking area. "I think that's her now."

Both turned to see a slender woman with long brown hair climb out of an older truck. Pulling out a small duffle, she slung it over her shoulder before walking toward them.

Jeramy Barrel, a longtime ranch hand, rushed to greet the woman.

"Seems you're right, Sam." Logan watched as the two greeted each other.

"I've seen her around. She played for one of the teams in the baseball league this summer. We talked a couple times. She's married to a local rancher."

Barrel ushered the woman around the crowd to where Sam and Logan stood. "Guys, this is Amanda Swanson. She's here to demonstrate barrel racing. Amanda, this is Samantha and Logan."

The three exchanged greetings with the women acknowledging they'd already met. Amanda looked past them into the arena.

"Is that Wyatt and Virgil?"

Barrel nodded. "Yep. Those boys have been competing since high school. Quit after college to run the ranch. They make a great team."

"Has a horse been selected for me?"

"Already saddled. You'll be riding Sugar, a real fine mare who raced the barrels until Virgil bought her for the ranch. I'll introduce you."

Amanda tipped her head at Sam and Logan before following Barrel to the barn. They turned back toward the arena to watch a handful of ranch hands show off their skills at calf roping.

"How have you been, Sam?"

She shrugged. "Good. Busy. The guest ranch brings in a lot of people who've never been on a working ranch. There's always lots to do, which is fine with me. You?"

"Same as you, except no guests to deal with. I wish the baseball league had lasted longer. Seems strange to have nothing to do on Saturday nights."

Chuckling, she nodded. "I hear you. I've volunteered to be on the parks board. The length of the playing season is one of the issues I'd like to bring up."

"Good to know."

Her brows drew together. "What?"

"Now I know someone with the inside scoop."

Gasps and some screams came from the crowd. Rushing to the fence, they saw one of the ranch hands sprawled on the ground, a steer standing about five feet away. Logan was about to climb over the fence to help when Wyatt and Virgil rushed in to check on the cowboy.

"He got his leg caught up in the rope," Sam said. "The steer must've dragged him around the arena before stopping."

A minute passed before the cowboy sat up, shook his head, then stood. With a lopsided smile on his face, he nodded at the enthusiastic crowd before Wyatt and Virgil helped him out the gate.

Barrel rushed in after them, drawing the attention of the onlookers. "A little excitement, folks. Be assured they'll take our cowboy to be checked out." He waited until the crowd settled down. "We have a special treat for you today. Amanda Swanson, from Kicking Horse Ranch, will be demonstrating the barrel racing event. Amanda is a regional and state champion. We're lucky to have her." Looking toward the gates, he saw her nod. "Let's welcome Amanda!"

Lifting their hats, the ranch hands whooped while the guests clapped. Entering through the gate, she took the barrels at a slow pace the first time around while Barrel narrated. She increased her speed for the second go-round, and drove even faster the third time.

Her demonstration finished without a glitch. Sliding to the ground, Amanda walked Sugar to the fence, giving the audience a close-up view of the horse and equipment used to race barrels. She patiently answered their questions.

Amanda's was the last demonstration of the day. She stayed to answer questions and greet the guests before walking Sugar back into the barn. Beginning to untack the mare, she stopped at the sight of Wyatt and Virgil walking toward her.

"Thanks for coming, Amanda. You did a great job out there." Wyatt nodded toward the arena.

"Anytime you need someone, give me a call. If I'm available, I'll be here."

Virgil inserted himself between her and Sugar, taking

over untacking the mare. "I know you have to get back to your husband."

She whispered her thanks, picked up her duffle, and continued to her truck.

"How is Mark?" Wyatt slid off the saddle and blanket, setting it on the rack.

Virgil shook his head. "As well as you'd think. He's got a long recovery, and still will never be a hundred percent."

Mark Swanson had been injured the previous year while training a stallion. Something had spooked the horse, triggering his flight instinct. The stallion reared back several times, his hooves landing on Mark. The rancher was lucky to be alive.

Virgil hung the bridle on its hook. "My last visit to their ranch was a week ago. He's in a wheelchair. It took him months to recover enough to get that far. It'll be a long time before walking on his own."

"Gotta be tough on Amanda."

"She's a strong woman. They've shared duties at the ranch for a long time." Virgil joined Wyatt as they left the barn. "They have two hired hands who've been with Mark for years. I believe the ranch will make it."

Logan drove his truck the short distance to the Kelman Ranch late that afternoon. He'd finished his work early to watch the rodeo. Now he faced dinner, a movie in his room, and bed.

"Saturday night and nowhere to go," he muttered, taking the last, slow curve toward home.

The ranch hands at Jake Kelman's spread were married, as was Jake, and Logan's brother, Quinn. The only single man, he usually tried to find someone from Whistle Rock to meet him in town. Barrel, Jimmy French, Brady Blackwolf, or sometimes, Sam. She usually arrived with other ranch hands. Still...

Slowing by the side of the road, he called Sam. "Hey, it's Logan."

"Hey, yourself. What's up?"

"Any chance you'd want to grab dinner in town?"

He could hear the chuckle in her voice. "Sure you don't want to go alone? You'd have a better chance of meeting someone if you're by yourself."

"Nah. I just need to get off the ranch for a bit. Are you up for it?"

"Sure. I'd like to get out myself."

"I'll pick you up at seven. That enough time to get ready?"

This time, she chuckled into the phone. "I've learned to be ready on short notice."

"Yeah. The life of a ranch hand."

"No kidding. Seven is fine. See you then."

Ending the call, he slid it into his pocket, glad he'd taken a chance.

"You have to be kidding." Logan took a bite of his double patty burger.

"Nope. The lady thought cutting her hair and wearing men's shirts would hide her womanness."

"Womanness? Is that even a word?"

"Not that I know about. My dad used it every time he told the story of her trying to get work at our ranch. To his credit, he hired her. It took three days to confirm she couldn't handle ranch work."

He looked over the top of his soda. "Then why'd she take the job?"

"She was looking for a cowboy to marry." Shaking her head, she took another bite of her cheeseburger.

"No kidding?"

"Happens more than you think. At least, I've seen it a lot between ranching and working for the rodeo production company. Most cowboys can spot one of these women a mile away."

Pushing away his empty plate, he leaned back in his chair. "Guess I never knew you worked for a rodeo company."

"Seven years. I attended community college for two years before being hired by Harmon & Sons."

Logan did a quick calculation. "So, you're about twenty-seven."

"Exactly twenty-seven. You're a youngster compared to me."

A smile broke across his face. "Hey, I'm no youngster. Besides, I'm a fast learner."

"I'll give you that. Jake says he's real glad to have you."

The band walked through the crowd to the stage, catching Sam and Logan's attention. Taking their places, they began the set with a song that had the crowd cheering. They clapped along.

The band slowed the tempo with the next song, an older country song. Sam sat forward in her chair, tapping her boots on the floor. Leaning toward her, Logan held out his hand.

"Let's dance."

She glanced at him as if he were nuts. Seeing the sincerity on his face, she grabbed his hand.

Chapter Two

Winters adjusted the hat given to him by Sheriff Garth Duggan. The deputy uniform fit as it should. The belt and boots were his, and he'd polished the latter until they shined.

The last step involved pinning the badge to his shirt. Not a simple task, getting it at the right location, not too high or low, and straight. It took a little longer than buttoning the shirt.

Staring at the bed, he surveyed what he'd laid out an hour earlier. The duty weapon, a Sig Sauer, belonged to him. Alongside it, he'd placed a flashlight, radio, extra magazines loaded with 9mm shells, and body armor. He'd be given anything else carried by a Riverdale County deputy when he arrived at headquarters.

Aiden stepped outside his rented house into full sun and a clear sky. Climbing into his newly purchased used Chevy truck, he took a longer route to the café where he'd meet the sheriff for an early breakfast. His first day as a law enforcement officer instead of the bounty hunter he'd been for several years.

The restaurant the sheriff selected was a diner at the south end of town. Aiden had been told it was owned by Duggan's aunt. The food filled their plates.

"I wanted to tell you a little about our department,

Winters." Duggan scooped another bite of eggs into his mouth, chewing absently as he washed the food down with coffee. "We've been contracted by the town of Brilliance to provide law enforcement services. There are twenty deputies who cover Riverdale County. Brilliance is the county seat, and where our main office is located. The area around this town is your main assignment, though you can be called to help out anywhere in the county. Which means, you're expected to travel when asked."

"Travel's no problem. I'll go wherever you need me."

"Good. I have a couple deputies who balk at traveling away from their main location, especially in winter. Thankfully, both are retiring this year." Garth smiled before taking several more sips of coffee. "My aunt does make the best coffee."

"Better than Lydia's?"

"Definitely. Lydia's strength is her baking. Brilliance Coffee & Bakery is a great place, but the coffee isn't the best."

Aiden thought he was right but didn't voice his vote. Swallowing the last of his coffee, he leaned back, waiting.

"Since you're using your own vehicle, you get reimbursed for each mile. Cindy, in our office, will go over all this along with your health benefits. Any questions for me?"

Aiden asked a few, satisfied with the answers. "Will Cindy provide the additional equipment needed?"

"There isn't much more than what you have, but yes. Cindy is the go-to person for all administrative issues.

Except for one." Duggan smiled. "Call me sheriff, or Garth, when it's just the two of us or around other deputies. Sheriff Duggan when we're around civilians."

"Works for me, Garth."

"Good. Your first assignment is to visit Whistle Rock Ranch." He stood, grabbing his hat. "Introduce yourself to those who don't know you."

"I believe I've met most of the people there." Aiden followed the sheriff outside.

"This trip is to let them know you've been hired. Wyatt and Virgil were two of your references. They sold me on hiring you."

This was new information for Aiden. "Then I'll thank them while I'm there."

"Good idea, Deputy. Stop by the office before you head home." The sheriff held out his hand. "Welcome to the department, Winters."

"Thank you, sir." Aiden stood on the sidewalk for several minutes, watching Garth drive off, and getting a better feel for that part of town.

When he'd been in Brilliance as a bounty hunter, most of his time was spent on Whistle Rock, meeting with the sheriff, and doing internet searches. This time, he'd be viewing the town through a different lens.

The trip to the ranch allowed him time to think about what he'd say to Wyatt and Virgil. He knew from the sheriff the two men were crucial in the decision to hire him. Aiden owed them more than a thank you, though those two inadequate words would have to do.

Whistle Rock Ranch came into view fifteen minutes after leaving town. The incredible summertime panorama across the ranch to the Tetons took his breath away.

The dry road stood in contrast to his last trip where the spring snow had turned to mud on the warmer days. He could see ranch hands, and what he supposed were guests, milling about the barns and corrals.

Parking the truck, he stepped out, straightening his uniform. Across the hood of the truck, he spotted Wyatt talking to a ranch hand near the barn. Virgil led a horse into the closest corral where several of the guests waited.

Aiden didn't want to interrupt either man. Deciding to stay out of sight, he leaned against the truck for several minutes, waiting for his chance. It came sooner than expected.

Wyatt spotted him as he approached from the parking area. "Hey, Deputy Winters. Good to see you." He stuck out his hand.

Aiden grabbed the outstretched hand. "I came to thank you and Virgil. It was your recommendations that convinced the sheriff to hire me."

"We just gave him the nudge he needed. Let's introduce you around so everyone knows of your change in status."

They walked first to the corral where Virgil demonstrated tacking up a horse. The crowd watched every move as he saddled the large animal, then slid the bit into the mouth before adjusting the bridle over the gelding's ears and head.

Shoving a boot into the left stirrup, he swung into the

saddle with an ease born from years of practice. The gelding had been trained well by him and Wyatt. Fourteen years old, calm, with a sweet disposition, anyone could ride him.

Finished with the demonstration, he rode to the fence and dismounted. "As guests, you don't have to worry about tacking up a horse. We'll have them ready for you to ride. If any of you want to learn, we'll be happy to teach you. Let Barrel know and arrange the training. Signups for trail rides posted for the week are already posted."

Virgil handed the reins to Barrel before leaving the corral to join Wyatt and Aiden. He held out his hand.

"It's a different look for you, Aiden. Congratulations."

"Thanks. Actually, I came to thank you and Wyatt for the recommendation."

Virgil waved a hand in the air. "Nothing more than you deserve. I'm glad Garth took our input seriously. Is today your first day on the job?"

"Sure is. I've been ready for a change. I took a chance and applied for the opening. How's everything around here?"

The three talked as Aiden scanned the area before stopping himself. He almost shook his head at the old habit of perusing his surroundings.

"Better than we could've ever hoped," Wyatt answered. "We have more guests than last year, and a waiting list for several weeks that are already filled." He looked to Virgil.

"Several activities have been added. If the growth continues, Gage will need to hire an assistant for next year."

"That's great news. I know how much all of you were

counting on this being a success."

"It's surpassed all of our expectations. Can you stay and have lunch with us?"

"Wish I could, Wyatt. There is time for me to meet any new ranch hands. Assuming someone's available to introduce me."

"There are just a couple," Virgil said. "I'll be glad to introduce you. It's always a good idea for them to know who the deputies are."

"One more bale and we're done for today, Quinn."

Logan unloaded the last of the bales of hay for storage in the stack yard. "That's it."

"Benny Takada will be here in about an hour. I'd like you to join us, Logan."

"He's your expert on Wagyu beef, right?"

"Yep. Benny's an expert on other ranch operations besides the beef. He'll be spending a couple nights with us before returning to Spokane."

"I thought he worked in Idaho." Logan closed the gate to the stack yard.

"He goes wherever there's work. The guy works seven days a week if he can. Benny doesn't do well with off time."

"A few days with me and he'll change his mind."

A deep laugh burst from Quinn. "Right. You spend most of your free time reading and playing video games."

"Hey. Sam and I went for burgers and music last

Saturday night."

"I bet it about killed you to ask if she wanted to tag along so you could get out of the house."

Logan walked behind Quinn as they stepped into his brother's mudroom. "It wasn't a date. Sam is a friend and nothing more." He leaned against the washing machine to remove his dirt-encrusted boots, setting them beside Quinn's.

"Are you sure?"

"Absolutely. Besides, Sam's older than me."

Quinn grabbed two water bottles from the refrigerator, handing one to his brother. "By how much?"

"Three years."

Recapping the bottle after a few swallows, Quinn set it on the counter. "That's nothing."

Logan was saved from answering when someone rapped on the front door. Walking past Quinn, he opened it to find a man he guessed to be Benny Takada.

"You must be Benny." Opening the door, he motioned him to enter.

"And you must be the brother. Logan, right?"

The men shook hands. "Right. Hope you don't believe everything my brother says."

"Not me." Benny smiled. "I'm pretty discerning."

"Glad to see you, Benny." Quinn joined them in the living room, clasping his friend on the shoulder. "What lies are you two sharing about me?"

"No lies. Just truths." Benny offered a wide smile.

"I'll take you at your word. How about something to

drink?"

"Water would be great, Quinn."

The foreman's house Jake built for Quinn and Abigail had been expanded during construction. Another two hundred square feet, mostly in the kitchen and living/dining room, had been added. It allowed more space for a mudroom and for meetings, such as the one with Benny.

Quinn handed out bottles of water before taking a seat at the dining room table. "So, what was so urgent about getting together?"

Opening his slim computer case, Benny pulled out a folder along with a few other documents. Passing one set to Quinn and the other to Logan, he let them read for a few minutes before both looked up, their faces taut.

"As you can see, we have a lot to talk about."

Chapter Three

"Sam! We need your help over here."

Virgil's shout had her running toward the corral where a small crowd gathered. It took seconds to determine why he called for her.

Jasmine, a teenager who accompanied another family to the ranch, lay on the ground in the closest corral. Virgil knelt beside her, checking her vitals while whispering words of encouragement.

He didn't need Sam for medical assistance. Since returning home from college, where he'd completed classes and hands-on medical training, he'd volunteered to be a backup EMT. The process took a while. He'd completed the paperwork to be an on-call employee and waited.

The hospital had called him a handful of times, usually when bad weather precluded an employee from making a shift and no one else was available. The arrangement allowed him to meet the crew at the site of an emergency. His skill had come in handy several times a year at the ranch. Sam dropped beside him.

"What happened?"

"Jasmine fainted. She should come around any second. I'd like her to see a woman beside her."

"Gotcha." Sam adjusted her location, placing a hand behind Jasmine's head while Virgil moved to the girl's other side. "She didn't hit her head, did she?"

"No. Dropped straight to the ground. We were talking through the trail ride and she fainted. All vitals are fine."

Jasmine moaned, her body shifting a little, one hand going to her forehead as her eyes opened. "What...?"

"Jasmine, it's Sam. Do you remember me?"

"Uh-huh. What happened?"

"You fainted."

"Fainted?" Jasmine pushed upward, succeeding with Sam's help.

"Just sit for a bit. Are you dizzy?"

"I don't think so."

"Do you have any idea why you fainted?"

Jasmine shook her head. A wave of dizziness struck her on a moan. It was then she noticed the people standing around, watching, and winced.

Sam seemed to read the girl's mind. "Don't worry about what happened. Everyone is just worried about you. Where is your friend?"

"Denise is with her parents in town. I didn't want to go." She shrugged. "This seemed more interesting. Can I stand up now?"

Sam glanced at Virgil, who'd been standing to the side, listening. "It's fine, Jasmine." He reached down to take one of her hands.

The crowd clapped when she stood, causing her face to flush. "This is so embarrassing."

"Sam's right. Don't worry about it. You know we'll need to tell the family you're with, and call your parents."

"Oh, please don't call my parents, Virgil. They'll insist I fly home. Plus, they'll insist I go to the hospital. It will ruin everything."

Chuckling, he stared at her for a moment, making a decision. "I'll talk to the family you came with and make a decision."

Jasmine's face lit up. "That's great. Thank you."

"We're done with the demonstration. Do you want me or Sam to walk you back to your cabin?"

"Thanks, but I'm pretty sure I can make it."

"Pretty sure isn't good enough," Virgil said.

"I'll walk with her." Sam sent an encouraging smile to Jasmine. "Be back in a few, Virgil."

He watched a minute to make certain the teenager would be all right before turning his attention to the guests who still stood around.

"Anyone have any questions?"

Sam sat with Jasmine for several minutes, checking her pupils once more. "Are you going to be okay?"

"Yeah. I feel silly. Especially since I have no idea why I fainted."

"None at all?"

Jasmine glanced away. "Well, I fainted at cheer practice back home."

Sam lowered herself onto a chair. "When was this?"

"A week or two before coming here."

"Did you go to emergency or have tests done?"

"No. My parents were getting ready for their long trip." She rolled her eyes. "They talked to our family doctor on the phone. They talked more about their trip than about me." Snickering, she dropped onto another chair. "I just get lightheaded. I tried to grab the corral rail this time but couldn't get to it."

"You aren't going to like this, but we should go to the hospital and talk to a doctor." Sam stood, taking a few steps toward the door.

"No!" Jasmine pursed her lips, lowering her voice. "I'd rather rest here."

"Not good enough, kiddo. I'm going to talk to Virgil."

"He'll agree with you."

"Probably. Fainting twice in a few weeks without a reason should be checked out. I'll come back and let you know what Virgil says."

Sam spotted him talking to a few of the guests. By the time she reached them, the crowd had dispersed.

"How's Jasmine?"

"All right, but we must take her to the hospital." Sam told him what she'd learned from Jasmine. "I can take her, Virgil. There's no need for both of us to go."

"I'd appreciate it, Sam. Doc Mason should be in emergency. Do you know who he is?"

"We've met. He was on the baseball team for the hospital. A real good player."

28

"Yeah. He chewed us up with his pitching. Do you need help with Jasmine?"

Sam chuckled. "She can walk fine. I'll fetch her and be off."

"Let me know what the doc says."

"Will do."

The emergency room didn't buzz with the normal crazy chaos Logan expected. Helping the injured ranch hand, he moved at a slow pace toward the attendant at the desk. He spoke before she could.

"We need to see the doctor as soon as possible."

Lifting her head, she did a slow perusal of the ranch hand, wincing at the blood seeping from the temporary bandage across his neck and around one arm. She noted his chin lolled against his chest.

"Is he awake?"

"Barely."

"What happened?"

"The tractor tipped over while he was driving. How long before we can get in to see the doctor?"

"A few minutes. Does he have insurance?"

Logan reached into a pocket, tossing the man's wallet on the desk. "It's in there."

While they waited, Doctor Mason Nagle walked out from the examination area. "Logan, right? Looks like your man needs our attention."

"That he does."

"Come on back." Mason glanced at the female clerk, who let out a sigh but said nothing.

As the door closed behind them, Logan heard a familiar voice. Glancing through the slight slit in the curtains as he passed the first cubicle, he smiled. Sam stood next to a bed, holding the hand of a younger girl.

"We'll put your man in here. What's his name?"

"Earl."

Placing him on the bed, Mason took a quick look at the injuries. "Earl, can you hear me?"

"Ye...yeah." His voice was thin and weak. "We'll need an X-ray. It appears your collarbone is broken. I believe your arm is all right, but you have a concussion."

"Hmmm..."

Mason looked at Logan. "I'll need you to wait in the front. As soon as I know the extent of his injuries, I'll let you know."

"Thanks, Doc. You're in good hands, Earl."

The ranch hand's reply was a guttural groan.

Leaving the cubicle, he stopped outside the one where he'd spotted Sam. He heard her voice. Pulling the curtain back, he saw a nurse tending to the patient. Looking to her side, Sam saw him.

"Logan. What are you doing here?"

"The same as you. I brought in an injured ranch hand."

"This is Jasmine. One of our guests. I'll be back in a minute, Jasmine."

The two moved to the waiting room. Neither sat down, believing they'd return to the emergency room.

"Who's the girl?"

"A guest at the ranch." Sam sent a quick look toward the emergency door. "Jasmine came with another family. She fainted during Virgil's demonstration of what to expect on a trail ride. When I accompanied her back to the cabin, she confessed to fainting a few weeks ago."

"Any reason?"

"That's why we're here. I hope Mason can find something that might be causing her to collapse."

"What about the family?"

"The one who brought her to the ranch went to town today. They know nothing yet. Virgil's deciding whether to tell them or call her parents. Jasmine mentioned her folks being on an extended vacation, which could make it hard."

"Wait. Her parents sent her with others so they could go on vacation alone?"

Sam's mouth drew into a tight line. "Seems so. What brought you here?"

"One of the ranch hands tipped the tractor, trapping him underneath. Doc is checking him out."

"He's lucky to be alive."

"I know. With what I understand so far, he's going to be laid up for a few weeks."

Staring at her boots, Sam shook her head while shoving both hands into the back pockets of her jeans. "That's tough. I know Quinn runs the ranch on a tight budget."

"We'll be all right. Jake mentioned asking Virgil to borrow a man as a short-time replacement."

"Or woman." She smiled.

"Right. Except you're the only woman, and we know how much Virgil depends on you. Do you want to get some coffee?"

"I'd love a cup, but I should stick close."

"No problem, Sam. I'll get a cup from the vending machine. Black?"

"Not a chance. I take sugar and cream. Can't stand it without something to cut down the bitter taste."

"Yes, ma'am." He gave a mock salute before leaving to find the machine.

Sam watched him go, a smile touching the corners of her mouth. Logan was a good-looking guy, and one of the nicest men she'd ever known. A great guy to hang out with. His good humor never changed, which suited her fine.

Her mind traveled to another man, and her smile faded. He'd been the complete opposite of Logan. She hadn't seen him in years, and hoped to never run into him again.

Chapter Four

Jonah Bonner shoved back from his computer, eyes aching from hours of work on today's presentation. The audience would pick apart his numbers and suggestions. They would be relentless, the same as they'd been when he was a boy.

The Bonner family was tougher than any bank loan committees he'd faced. Rightly so. What he'd show them would indicate whether they should continue some aspects of the ranch and consider closing others. The ranch provided a livelihood for over two dozen people, including the entire Bonner clan.

Jonah stood, raising both arms for a long stretch. He'd been lax in his exercise routine last week. His early morning run of six miles had been cut to four. He hadn't ridden his horse in days, and counted five hours of sleep as an excellent night.

The printer kicked out the last of the documents. A copy for each person, plus one extra. This wouldn't require a PowerPoint presentation. The documents in his hand would be enough.

"You ready, bro?" Jonah's younger brother, Gage, stood in the doorway.

"All set."

Their offices were located upstairs at the back of the large lodge, while their parents' and Wyatt's were downstairs. Anson Bonner, the patriarch, had stepped back after a heart attack, appointing his oldest son to take his place. Virgil had been appointed the foreman when his father, Jasper, faced severe medical issues, forcing him to cut back on work. They'd all be there, along with their mother, Margie, and Virgil's mother, Monica.

Jonah and Gage entered their father's office to the hum of conversation. As they took their seats, Jonah could make out enough words to know Wyatt was advocating for more hires. Anson countered the suggestion, saying they already had plenty of people.

"All right, gentlemen." Margie touched her husband's arm. "Jonah is here. Let's sit down and see the numbers."

Anson grumbled to himself while pulling out his chair. "Jonah, Gage. Glad you two could make it."

"We're right on time, Pop." Gage took a seat next to his mother.

Anson's mouth twisted as he checked the time. "I suppose you're right. Jonah, what do you have for us?"

Passing out the documents, Jonah sat next to his father. He waited for the others to look through the spreadsheets and read the executive page. It contained a summary and his recommendations. He saw that Wyatt scanned the spreadsheets quickly, moving within minutes to Jonah's summary. Virgil did the same.

Anson lifted his head, focusing hard on Jonah. "Start explaining."

Clearing his throat to hide a grin at his father's frosty voice, he looked around the table. "The numbers are holding up and expanding in most areas. Sales of trained horses are above last year, cattle prices are stable, and the numbers for the guest ranch are far above expectations."

Shuffling the documents, Jonah held up the summary. "As you can see, I'm recommending we add two cabins for the guest ranch operation. We've been booked to capacity so far this season, turning reservation requests down for most weeks. The numbers show four additional cabins could be supported, though I'm not sold on going that route. If the economy turns, so might reservations."

Jonah continued to the cattle operation before moving to the training and sale of horses, recommending modest changes for each. When finished, he looked around the table. He didn't notice dissent on their faces. A good sign. As usual, his father was the first to speak.

"I don't like the idea of building more cabins. Not even two."

Wyatt responded. "Two more and we'll be at the number we projected when we first discussed the guest operations."

Margie looked at her husband. "We all agreed to start slow, knowing we might have to turn people away. Additional cabins were included in the initial plan. I think two more makes sense." She turned toward Jonah. "Do the numbers suggest two more will be all we'll need?"

"The short answer is yes. Building more than that will require us to extend the electricity and water lines, which we won't have to do with just the two additional cabins."

Wyatt leaned forward, resting his arms on the table.

"So that could be the limit of what we'll build?"

Jonah nodded. "The costs go up considerably by adding more than two. My thoughts are we should cap it at two more and work within the number of spots available."

Gage set down his copies. "I agree with Jonah and Wyatt. The outdoor activities I run are close to but not yet at capacity. Two more cabins might not fill them, but it's not going to hurt the adventure trips offered by the guest ranch."

Anson grumbled without voicing his dissent. Most in the room knew he'd made up his mind before seeing Jonah's numbers.

Wyatt looked at his closest friend. "What do you think, Virgil?"

"We always seem to keep the cabins full. Sometimes, they're full of guests. Other times with our extended family and friends. There are also instances of people calling at the last minute. If two more work into the numbers, I'd say we go ahead with them."

It took several more minutes of discussion before a vote was taken. Anson said nothing when the majority sided with Jonah.

Compared to the addition of two cabins, the remainder of the meeting continued with few disagreements. Ninety minutes flew by before they dispersed to continue their duties around the ranch. Wyatt caught up with Jonah, flinging an arm over his brother's shoulders.

"Great job, bro. When does construction start?" He dropped his arm to his side.

Jonah glanced over his shoulder, confirming their father was nowhere near them. "Don't pass this around, but I already approved plans. The contractor and his crew will start the first of the week."

"Way to speed things up. Anything I can do?"

"You have enough to do without taking on more work. Plus, I've already gotten most of the project in place."

"Understood." Wyatt clasped his brother's shoulder. "If you need anything, let me know."

"Thanks. I'll keep you posted on progress."

News about the addition of two more cabins spread fast. The ranch hands, and even some guests, applauded the expansion. One couple took the time to explain to Sam how they'd wanted to invite another couple, but the ranch was booked by then. They were already planning to make reservations for two cabins the following summer.

She'd passed the information along to Virgil, who told Wyatt, who sat down with Jonah to give his brother all the feedback he'd heard. No one thought to tell Anson.

"Sam!" Barrel jogged toward her, stopping a few feet away. "You have a phone call."

"That's odd. My phone didn't ring."

"It's on the phone in the barn. He's on hold."

"Hold?"

"Yeah. It's some guy. Wouldn't tell me what it was about."

A knot formed in her stomach. She didn't move. It was as if her boots were planted in the ground.

"Uh, you gonna take the call?"

"Did he ask for me specifically?"

"Sure did. He wanted Samantha."

"Hmmm." She glanced down at the ground before lifting her gaze to Barrel. "Do you mind telling him I'm not available?"

"I can do that. Are you in some kind of trouble?"

"No." She shook her head. "No trouble."

"You'd just rather not speak to this particular man?"

"Yeah."

"Got you covered, Sam. And don't worry, I won't give him your mobile number."

"Thanks, Barrel. I owe you."

He waved her off as he headed back to the barn.

The knot stayed in her stomach until close to dinner. Jake Kelman, Quinn, and Logan joined the Whistle Rock ranch hands. Logan filed into the buffet line behind Sam, heaping slices of roast beef, potatoes, gravy, and vegetables onto his plate.

"Are you sitting with your brother?" Sam asked as they stood next to each other with full plates.

A smile spread across his face. "I'd rather sit with a pretty lady."

"Guess you better go find one."

"I already know one. Now, find us a couple seats."

She did. Two seats were open across from Virgil and his wife, Lily. Next to them were Wyatt and his wife, Daisy. The last were enjoying an hour together while Wyatt's parents watched their infant son, Reece.

"You know how Pop is." Wyatt glanced around, lowering his voice. "He isn't going to like anything one of his sons comes up with."

"I know." Virgil shrugged. "I thought with the success of the guest ranch he might start showing an open mind."

"Anson and open mind don't go together in the same sentence." Wyatt slid more potatoes into his mouth.

Daisy looked at Lily before each chuckled. Sam and Logan stayed silent. They all knew how stubborn Anson Bonner could be. Everyone for miles around knew about the cantankerous rancher who'd built Whisper Rock into a formidable competitor in horse breeding and cattle. Now, his sons and foreman were enjoying success as a guest ranch, dragging the older rancher along with them.

Wyatt looked across the table at Sam. "What are your thoughts about how the guest ranch is doing?"

Setting her fork down, she leaned back in her chair. "Judging by what the guests tell me, it's a real success. I hear you're going to build two more cabins."

Wyatt nodded. "We got approval today."

"I believe it's good to strike while you're hot." She smiled. "According to several guests, Whistle Rock Ranch is becoming the place to stay in western Wyoming."

Virgil nodded. "That's good to hear, Sam."

Shrugging, she took another bite of potatoes smothered in rich, dark brown gravy. "Beth and Abbie make the best gravy. Whosever's recipe it is, I want a copy."

Everyone chuckled. Logan stopped eating to stare at her. "You cook?"

One derisive brow lifted. "Of course, I cook. I'm not one of these women who acts as if making a meal is beneath her. It's not like I could survive on those tiny premade meals." She snorted at the idea.

"Prove it."

"What?"

"Come up to the house sometime soon and cook for us."

"For you, Quinn, Abbie, Beth, and Jake?" She laughed.

"Sure. Why not?"

"I said I cook. Not that I'm great at it. Jeez." Forking a slice of beef, she chewed it, hoping Logan would let the idea go.

"Sunday. Neither of us works. You'd have all the time needed to make Sunday supper. Tell me what you need and I'll buy it."

Aware those across the table were listening, she set down her fork. "Fine. I'll grill six steaks. Corn on the cob. Don't husk them. Idaho russet potatoes. Not those teensy ones in the store. I'll bring the salad, bread, and dessert."

He stared at her again. "You're really going to cook for us?"

"Heck yes. I refuse to back down from a cooking challenge. Besides, I heard Beth has an incredible kitchen." Sam smiled at Daisy and Lily. "And if I mess something up, Abbie and Beth will be there to bail me out."

Chapter Five

The plan to barbecue at the Kelman Ranch almost got scuttled when a thunderstorm broke loose as Sam seasoned the steaks. The men grabbed the combination smoker with grill, placing it just inside the barn. While Jake and Quinn leveled it, Logan raked away stray hay and stall bedding.

The potatoes were already in the oven. She'd placed the salad in the refrigerator, and the bread and pies on the kitchen counter. Beth and Abbie had set the table, placed out glasses, and pulled serving bowls from the cupboards. The next task involved avoiding the rain while carrying a platter of steaks to the barn. The last involved dashing through the open barn doors, avoiding the mud and growing number of puddles.

"Hold these." Sam handed the platter to Logan, who lifted the plastic wrap. "Hey, leave those alone."

"Checking to see if you seasoned them correctly."

Removing her coat's hood, she lifted a brow. "Sure you were."

Ignoring his laugh, she lifted the lid of the grill. The men had seasoned it and turned on the flame.

Logan stood on the other side of the grill, watching and commenting as the steaks cooked. "Don't you think they're done?"

She tested them. "Another minute."

"All you did was touch them."

"Hey. I watched Bobby Flay do it on TV. He knows all about his stuff."

"I hope so. Those steaks cost me a week's pay."

"Not hardly." She tested the steaks again. "A few more seconds."

Logan held out the platter. "I like mine rare."

"I know. You've told me about a dozen times."

"Quinn likes his medium."

"Right." Placing two steaks on the platter, she waited another minute before adding four more steaks alongside the others. A minute later, she added the last steak to the platter. "That'll do it." She looked at Logan. "There are six of us. Why a seventh steak?"

"Benny Takada, a good friend of Quinn's, is joining us." He looked toward the road. "That's him now."

A truck, its tires, front, and sides covered in mud, stopped not far from them. A man about Quinn's age with black hair, dark brown eyes, and a ruddy complexion got out.

Logan motioned for Benny to follow him and Sam into the house. The three rushed to the door and dashed inside.

"That's quite a storm." Benny placed his hat on a hook and slid out of his coat. "How are you doing, Logan?"

"Great." He turned toward Sam, who'd walked to the counter to set down the platter. "Sam, this is Benny Takada, one of the premier Wagyu beef specialists in the country. Benny, Samantha Miller. She works at Whistle Rock Ranch."

42

They exchanged greetings, Benny moving to the counter to check out the steaks. "Those look great. What can I do to help?"

Sam glanced around. "You could place the corn in the serving bowl next to the stove."

"You're brave. I've never been able to cook corn on the cob."

"Most people overcook it. What some don't realize is you can eat them right after removing them from the stalk in the field. You don't need to cook them. Boil water and add a half cup or so of milk. Turn off the heat, then place the shucked ears in the pan. Let them sit a few minutes, until they're warm, and serve them."

"That's it?"

"Yep. My aunt and uncle used to grow acres of corn on their farm. Their field produced the best corn I've ever tasted."

"Good to know. I'll give your method a try the next time I cook corn." He moved the bowl next to the platter of steaks.

Sam looked at him. "You might want to wait until you've tasted today's corn before deciding."

"I'm sure it will be great."

"Hey, Benny. When did you get here?" Quinn held out his hand.

"Five minutes." He clasped the outstretched hand. "Sam was telling me her secret for preparing corn."

Quinn looked at her. "You have a secret, Sam?"

She smirked. "All women have secrets, Quinn. You

43

should know that by now."

"How long will you be staying here, Benny?" Sam set down her coffee, picking up a plate with a generous slice of peach pie. Taking a bite, she felt a small surge of satisfaction at the burst of flavors.

"This is wonderful pie, Sam. Why didn't I know you were an accomplished cook?" Beth slid a fork under a small piece, slipping it into her mouth.

"I don't usually have time to cook. When I do, it's for me."

"What happens when you make a full pie?" Abbie asked.

"I eat it." Sam laughed along with the others.

Logan watched her, the same as he had since she'd arrived earlier that afternoon. Something about her affected him in a way he'd never experienced. It was ridiculous. She was good-looking. His mother would've called her cute. Of course, his mother always thought of herself as beautiful. She preferred the word stunning, though Logan had never understood the difference.

"Did you know Sam could cook, Logan?"

He shook his head at Beth. "Not a clue."

Jake stood, cutting himself another piece of pie. "Good idea to bring two pies, Sam. I believe they'll be empty by the time you head home."

"Thanks, Jake." Sam shot a look at Logan, expecting

him to make a comment, making everyone laugh. He didn't. Nor did he cut another slice for himself. Odd, given what she'd witnessed when he ate at the ranch.

"Is this your mother's recipe?" Abbie refilled her cup with steaming coffee.

"My father's. He was a terrific baker. My mother cooked the meals, and he made desserts, muffins, cookies, banana bread, gosh…just about anything you find at a bakery, my father could make. He always did great at the county fair."

Benny took another slice of pie for himself. "Where'd you grow up, Sam?"

"Oklahoma. My parents own a small ranch. With the amount of food they raise, it could be called a farm. Pop trained horses and raised a few head of Angus cattle. We never had a lot of money, but we didn't need much. Where'd you grow up, Benny?"

"Seattle, mostly. My parents wanted me to be a doctor. A lawyer would've been all right, too. Broke their hearts when I wanted to raise cattle." He chuckled. "I thought they'd disown me. I told them it was their fault for sending me to Japan for part of my schooling. If they hadn't insisted I go, I never would've learned about cattle and Wagyu beef."

Sam leaned forward, resting her arms on the table. "What do they think of your choice now?"

"I'm a genius."

She laughed with everyone else. "I just bet you are."

"I sure hope you are, Benny." Jake set his empty plate aside. "We've invested a good deal in those cattle."

"Another year and you'll get your investment back,

Jake. There's a real market for the beef in big cities. It's catching on in smaller communities. You're in a good spot to take advantage of the trend."

Beth's brows scrunched together. "Trend?"

Benny nodded. "Yes. The whole farm-to-market trend. Chefs want to offer local food. Their customers like the idea of ordering items sourced from the region where they live."

"Or visit," Quinn said.

"Right. Vacationers drive much of the demand." Rising, Benny filled a glass with water, drinking every ounce before filling it again.

Logan stood, picking up empty plates and carrying them into the kitchen. He'd gotten into the habit of doing the dishes when eating with Quinn and Abbie or Jake and Beth. They cooked, he cleaned. Always seemed a good deal to him.

"Let me help." Sam opened the dishwasher, loading plates and utensils.

"You sure surprised everyone with your cooking."

"My mother thought I'd better have a skill besides working horses and cattle. I spent a few hours every week cooking, sewing, all the stuff she knew. It was worth the time."

"I agree. Everything was great, Sam. I owe you a dinner out."

"You don't owe me anything, Logan. It was fun cooking for more than just me."

"I'm surprised you cook at all with the meals Beth and Abbie prepare at Whistle Rock."

"I don't cook often. Every few weeks, or if I'm late for breakfast. Or if I just want some time alone. You know how it is."

Logan nodded. "I believe I do. There are nights I get into my truck and drive. Nowhere in particular in mind. Just drive. Sometimes, I wonder if the best decision would be to return home."

"To your mother?" Closing the dishwasher door, she leaned against the counter. She knew the story of why he'd come to the Kelman Ranch to find his half-brother. At the time, Quinn had no idea about Logan's existence.

"I might go to my father's place. He's getting older and could use the help."

"I'll miss you, Logan. You're about the only man I can meet up with for dinner and dancing."

"I haven't made up my mind, Sam. It's something to consider. Don't you ever think about going home?"

"To Oklahoma?"

He nodded.

"For a visit, but not to live. My parents sold the ranch last year. They bought a house in town with three bedrooms and two baths on an oversized lot. Mom has a garden and Pop sits on the porch with the neighbors. Every so often, he bakes something." Her small smile held a hint of wistfulness. "I'd never be able to move back for good."

"Never say never, Sam."

"You're right. I'll probably inherit their house. And Pop's rocking chair."

They both laughed at the picture Sam painted.

"Logan! Sam! Get out here."

The light moment turned serious as both ran through the living room to the front porch. They stood frozen alongside the others, watching flames lick the sides of a barn at Whistle Rock Ranch.

"I have to get down there." Sam pulled keys from a pocket as she ran to her truck. Jumping inside, she wasn't surprised to see Logan slide in on the passenger side.

Chapter Six

The fire didn't look quite as bad as it had from the Kelmans' front porch. Pulling to a stop away from the burning barn, Sam and Logan jumped out as Jake and the others parked beside them.

"Virgil's over there." Sam pointed before running toward him. She didn't have to look over her shoulder to know the others followed. "What happened?"

Virgil swiped an arm across his forehead. "We don't know. One of the guests spotted it. Wyatt contacted the fire department. They'll be here soon."

Jake stood beside Virgil, watching the ranch hands work to put out the fire. "What do you want me to do?"

"Right now, stay back and wait. Wyatt is directing the ranch hands. Barrel is helping him. They've already put out the majority of it."

Sam watched the ranch hands spray water on the blaze. "Good that it's one of the smaller barns."

Virgil nodded. "Glad we put in the additional water spigots last fall."

The sound of sirens cut through the sounds of the fire. Jake ran toward the fire truck, motioning where they should park. Two sheriff department vehicles pulled in several feet behind them. Sheriff Garth Duggan exited one while Deputy Aiden Winters got out of the other. Both men ran toward Virgil.

Garth shoved his hat back from his forehead. "Do you know how it started?"

Virgil shook his head. "No. Has the fire investigator been notified?"

"The fire captain usually contacts them when they get the call for help. I have no idea how long it will take for him to get here."

Beth spoke to Abbie. "Let's make coffee and put out sandwiches for everyone."

"I'll help." Sam followed them to the kitchen.

Logan watched her leave, wondering at the strange emptiness in his chest. The feeling confused him, but this wasn't the time to think about the odd sensation.

No one noticed the slender woman, her blonde ponytail swinging, as she ran toward the group. "Virgil?"

"Mrs. Maddox. What can I do for you?"

Those who worked on the ranch knew the young widow had booked three consecutive weeks. She'd arrived alone with more luggage than necessary, even for an extended stay.

Glancing around the group, she spotted the sheriff and the deputy who'd introduced himself to the guests a few days earlier. Swallowing the lump in her throat, she forced herself to explain.

"I may have seen who started the fire."

This caught everyone's attention. Aiden studied her face before stepping forward.

"Laurel Maddox, right?"

"You have a good memory, Deputy Winters."

Aiden shot a look at the sheriff, who motioned for him to go ahead. "Let's talk over here." He motioned for her toward the lodge's front porch. Once there, he took out a pad and pen from a pocket, holding them to his side. A reminder of how he still clung to a few old-school habits.

"What did you see?"

Worrying her lower lip, she glanced toward the fire before meeting his questioning gaze. "I believe someone started the fire."

"All right. Tell me what you saw."

"Well, I was sitting on the porch of my cabin. I'm in number five, which gives me a great view of the barns and corrals. I'd just made tea, and..." She shook her head. "Sorry, you don't care about that. Guess I'm nervous."

"Take your time, Mrs. Maddox. We have plenty of it."

"Please, call me Laurel."

"All right. Laurel it is. Tell me what you saw."

"A man went into the barn. But it was more the way he went inside."

"What do you mean?"

"He stopped and looked around. It's a guess, but it was like he wanted to make sure no one saw him." She released a shaky breath. "He was dressed all in black. That's not too unusual except he had one of the beanies on his head."

"A knit watch cap?"

"Right. It was pulled down low."

"Color."

"From the porch, it looked black. I remember thinking

about him being a cliché of characters I've seen on television." She fell silent as if recalling what she saw.

Aiden waited a minute before interrupting her thoughts. "Did you recognize him?"

"What? Oh yes. I mean, no." She shook her head. "I didn't recognize him."

"And you're sure it was a man?"

Her brows drew together. "Well...I was. I suppose it could've been a woman."

"We'll figure that out later. Did you see him start the fire?"

"No. But when he ran out, it wasn't long before I saw flames."

"What did you do when you saw the flames?"

"I ran to the cabin where Virgil and Lily live. He took care of things from there."

"All right, Laurel. Which way did he run when he left the barn?"

"That was also strange. He ran around the barn and disappeared."

"He didn't run to one of the cabins?"

"No. Around the barn toward the back."

Aiden thought a moment before continuing. "Is that when you saw the flames?"

"Maybe a minute later."

"That's when you ran to Virgil's cabin."

Her head bobbed in a grave nod. "Yes."

"You didn't tell Virgil about the man?"

"I didn't connect the fire to him until later." A cloud

crossed her features. "Seems obvious now."

He waited a bit before sliding the pad and pen into a pocket. "Don't beat yourself up. You figured it out pretty fast compared to most people. Doesn't count the people who don't want to get involved and wouldn't have gone for Virgil. People are a strange bunch, Laurel."

"How well I know."

Logan thought he'd prefer to work outside, helping the ranch hands do whatever the fire chief directed. Wyatt and Virgil had other plans for him and a few of the guests who volunteered their time.

Beth put him to work alongside Sam, fixing sandwiches for the entire crew. Abbie and Benny assembled large bowls of macaroni, Ceasar, and fruit salads, while Daisy, with Reece sleeping nearby, and Lily, baked cookies. The biggest challenge was rescuing fresh, warm chocolate chip and oatmeal cookies from the hands of those working in the kitchen.

"Do you believe one of the guests may have started the fire?" Sam glanced at Logan as she smeared mustard on another slice of sourdough bread.

"If it was arson, anyone could've started the fire. Including a ranch guest." Layering meat and cheese on the bread, he handed it to Margie Bonner, who added lettuce and a tomato slice before sliding it down the counter to Monica Redstar for packaging. "The fire inspector will be able to tell if it was an accident, freak occurrence, or arson."

Monica stopped wrapping sandwiches. "If one of our guests started the fire, I hope he's given a long prison sentence. He won't be able to do it again if he's locked up."

"I agree with you," Margie said. "The sooner he's arrested, the sooner we'll feel safe."

Sam looked at Margie. "Do you think he'd torch guest cabins?"

"An arsonist will strike anywhere. They don't discriminate, Sam."

Except for the sounds of food preparation, the room fell silent. When the kitchen door opened, it was as if someone dropped a ceramic bowl on the tile floor, startling everyone.

Wyatt stepped a few feet inside before stopping at the lack of noise. "Is something wrong?"

His mother, Margie, turned to face him. "We were discussing what to do with the arsonist."

"Bet that was an interesting conversation." He moved next to Daisy. "Fresh cookies?"

"Yes, and don't even think about stealing one."

"Dang. Well, I'm here to let you know the fire truck and crew are leaving in about fifteen minutes. If the food is ready, I'd like to start handing it out to the firefighters. Next to the ranch hands and guests."

"No problem, boss." Beth looked at those in the kitchen. "Let's place the food on the tables outside."

The firefighters were ravenous. Sam didn't know if the empty bellies came from working the ranch's fire or if the men were always starving. She suspected the latter.

"How're you doing, Sam?"

She recognized the voice and smiled. "I'm doing fine, Brady. You?"

"I'm always good." He reached for a sandwich, stopping when Sam stilled his hand. "What?"

"Are you here as a ranch hand or a Splendor firefighter?"

"Which one allows me to eat now?"

She chuckled. "You are something."

"So, which one?"

"Firefighter."

"Great." He grabbed a sandwich and a package of cookies. "For the record, I did work this as a volunteer firefighter."

"Never a doubt."

His face lit with one of his devastating smiles, sending Sam's insides into a tizzy. She watched as he walked away, shaking her head. Brady Blackwolf, Virgil's cousin, ranch hand, firefighter, and one of Splendor's most eligible bachelors.

"Trouble, trouble, trouble," she muttered.

"Talking to yourself, Sam?"

She winced, hoping Logan hadn't heard her. "You know how it is."

"Not sure I do, but if talking to yourself helps, I'd say go for it."

Chuckling, she held up a sandwich. "Have you eaten yet?"

Logan shook his head. "I'll wait until everyone else eats.

Besides, I know where to find the fixin's."

Sam handed out a wrapped sandwich to another firefighter. An older man she didn't recognize. He wore a patch that read, *Captain*.

"Salads and cookies?"

Raising his head, Sam noticed his weary eyes. "Captain?"

"Uh, yes. Cookies. No salad."

She held them out. "Thanks for all you and your men do."

A slight smile appeared. The effort had Sam reevaluating his age. Instead of forty, maybe closer to thirty-five.

Right behind him came the ranch hands, and a few guests. She knew they'd all eaten dinner earlier, but if they helped with the fire, they deserved more food. At the end of the line stood Aiden Winters. Next to him was Laurel Maddox, the woman who thought she'd spotted the person who started the fire.

"Hello, Sam."

"Deputy. Mrs. Maddox. We have ham, beef, and chicken sandwiches, salad, and cookies."

He motioned for Laurel to go ahead of him. She had a chicken sandwich without salad or cookies. Aiden took all three.

No one else came forward. Sam turned toward Logan.

"Guess that's all. If we missed anyone, they'll have to come to the kitchen."

"So, I can take what I want?"

Sam chuckled. "Whatever you want. I'm pretty certain everyone in the kitchen has already eaten."

She picked up a beef sandwich. Unwrapping it, she took a big bite. Chewing, Sam looked up at him. "Aren't you going to eat?"

"Sure am. Just wanted to be the very last one."

They ate in silence until each opened a package of cookies. Sam nibbled at hers while Logan finished his in a few bites.

"Well, guess I need to hitch a ride home." Logan nodded toward the Kelman Ranch.

"I'll take you up the hill."

He looked at her for a while before shaking his head. "Nah. It's a beautiful night. I'm going to walk."

Logan started off without a goodbye. Not saying another word until he was about fifty yards away.

"Hey, Sam."

"Yeah?"

"Let's grab dinner and go dancing this Friday."

Her answer popped right out. "Sounds good to me."

Chapter Seven

"I really appreciate both of you coming with me to look at the space." Laurel Maddox fidgeted with her purse strap as Daisy drove toward the empty retail space near Lydia's coffee and baked goods shop. She'd expected to bring Reece with her, but Margie volunteered to watch him.

"I'm not sure there's anything I can add to what Daisy thinks. She's the expert on what goes on in Brilliance." Sam glanced at the buildings on the main street. Given the long days at the ranch, it wasn't often she saw them during the day.

"You're straightforward, Sam. Whatever your opinion is, I know it will be honest."

"You're right on that."

Laurel smiled. "You'd be surprised at the number of people who aren't comfortable telling you how they really feel about something. You aren't one of them."

Sam's mouth twisted into a wry grin. "I don't know if that's good or bad."

"It's good," Laurel answered. "This is a huge step for me. You and Daisy will offer different perspectives, but each will be honest."

"Are you planning to buy a building or rent one?" Daisy asked.

"I'm not sure. The one we'll see today is for sale."

Daisy glanced over at Laurel. "Who's the owner?"

"It's a trust." She opened a file folder to scan the details on the first document. "WJGB Trust."

Daisy shot her another quick look. "Say that again."

"WJGB Trust."

Snorting a chuckle, Daisy parked in front of the building Laurel wanted to see.

"What is it?"

Turning off the engine, Daisy grinned. "How convenient."

"What's convenient?" Sam asked.

"WJGB Trust stands for Wyatt Jonah Gage Bonner. It's one of at least three trusts Anson and Margie established. WJGB is for their sons. Wyatt told me one of the others is a charitable trust. I don't know what the others are for."

"Interesting," Laurel said. "I wonder why Anson and Margie are selling."

"Anson and Margie are probably the only two who know. This could be a good thing for you, Laurel."

"How's that?"

"Margie might be flexible with the price."

"And Anson?"

Daisy thought a moment. "Only Anson knows the answer to that. Are you ready to see it?"

"Absolutely."

A short, rotund woman with graying hair and a broad smile met them at the front door. "Good morning, ladies. I'm Juneau Jacobs, the listing agent."

After introductions, she unlocked the door. "Before you

go inside, I'd like to give you a little history. The building was built in 1935. It was a retail store below with a large apartment on the second floor. The last tenant was a cafe, open for twenty-five years before the owner retired. As you can see, the bank is on one side, and an office building on the other. Mostly, the tenants in that building are independent professionals, such as accountants, attorneys, land appraisers, and the like. Take your time looking around. The upstairs is open. I think you're going to like what you see."

"The building is for sale, correct?" Laurel asked.

"Yes. Though, the owners might be willing to offer a lease for the right tenant."

"With an option to purchase?"

"If they approve you as a tenant, I'm sure they'd be willing to consider an option. The first step is to decide if the space fits your needs." Juneau motioned for them to enter.

Seconds ticked by before Laurel voiced her first impression. "Oh, my. Look at all the beautiful woodwork."

Sam's gaze moved over the space. "It doesn't look like much now, but there's a lot of potential."

Laurel looked around, giving a slow nod. "You're right."

"And the soda counter," Sam added. "Did you ever eat here, Daisy?"

"Many times. It was the place to hang out during junior high and high school. Parents who worked would have their children meet them here."

Laurel walked to the marble soda counter, running her

hand over the surface. "A gathering place."

Sam stared at the round stools, each one covered in new black vinyl. "Wouldn't it be something if you were able to combine your flower shop with the soda joint?"

"What a great idea, Sam." Daisy walked behind the counter. "There are plenty of shelves. Someone must've maintained everything."

Juneau joined them. "The tenant retired just a few years ago. He and his wife kept the place immaculate."

"Oh, I remember them," Daisy said. "Mr. and Mrs. Goldberg. They had a son two years older than me. Very smart, but also very quiet. I wonder whatever happened to him."

Juneau smiled. "Isaac graduated from law school last year. He's with a big firm in Seattle. I believe the Goldbergs are still deciding whether to sell their home in Brilliance and join him on the coast or keep their place and travel."

"I'd love to have a choice like that someday." Sam's voice held a wistful tone.

"The owners couldn't decide what to do with the building. One wanted to sell. The other preferred to find another tenant. Preferably one who'd reopen the café. They finally came to a decision to sell. It's been on the market less than a week. Go on upstairs. I was up there a few days ago. It's quite impressive."

All three younger women ran their hands over the wood banister as they took the stairs to the second level. Reaching the top, Laurel spotted a door to her right.

"This must be the entry. It's a little odd looking." Laurel

gripped the knob.

"I hope the inside is as good as downstairs," Sam said.

Turning the knob, Laurel led them inside. "Wow. This is nice."

"Really nice," Sam said.

"And huge." Daisy walked farther inside and stopped. "The kitchen is incredible. Everything looks brand new."

"I wonder how many bedrooms." Laurel walked down a hallway. Sam followed a moment later. Daisy continued her scrutiny of the kitchen, living room, and dining room.

"One large bedroom and two smaller ones. Two bathrooms." Laurel walked to the front window and looked out. "There's a park across the street."

Daisy joined her. "The city organizes different events which are held there. Concerts, mainly. The baseball fields are a few blocks away. The ranch has a team. They did pretty good last year, and are doing even better this year."

Laurel returned to the kitchen and opened the cabinets and drawers. "There are pots and pans, plates, bowls, utensils. This is an amazing apartment."

"You could live here," Daisy said.

Laurel shrugged. "It's a little large for one person."

"Then rent it out. You might get enough to cover most of the rent for the flower shop." Daisy pulled out one of the stools and sat down. "I like this high counter."

"I do, too." Laurel took a seat beside her.

"So, what do you think?" Sam asked.

"Well, it's much larger than I need. Which means the rent will probably be more than I can afford."

Daisy slid off the st   nds as if it's time to find out."

Logan helped Jake and Quinn unload another stack of lumber near the site of the destroyed barn. As an employee of Whistle Rock, Jake had an obligation to help prepare the area for a replacement barn. Quinn and Logan didn't have the same obligation, yet both had volunteered.

Grabbing three bottles of water, Logan kept one, tossing the other two to Jake and Quinn. Twisting off the cap, he took a long swallow.

"The barn will take about a week if everyone puts in a few extra hours every night." Logan drained the rest of the water before taking a seat on the tailgate of his truck.

"There are a good number of guests who are helping out," Jake said.

"Plus, Aiden Winters is here with a couple other deputies." Quinn drank the last of his water. "Benny felt bad about having to leave."

Jake took a seat next to Logan. "How long will he be gone?"

"A week." Quinn tossed his bottle onto a pile of material to be recycled. "He'll come back here when he's finished."

"Another Wagyu beef rancher?" Jake asked.

"I didn't ask, but that is his specialty."

"Hey, boys. Are any of you hungry?" Sam approached, holding a large box in one hand and a bag filled with bottles of water in the other.

"What are you offering?" Logan flashed her a smile.

She peeked inside. "Let's see. Pizza, pizza, and, oh yes...pizza."

Logan laughed. "Pizza all around."

Handing the box to Jake, she set down the bag, taking a water bottle for herself. "The pizza was donated to us. Amanda and Mark Swanson brought them by. He said they were real sorry they couldn't help."

"That's the woman who demonstrated barrel racing, right?" Logan took another large bite of pizza.

Sam nodded. "They were returning from another of Mark's doctor visits in Hobson." She nibbled at her pizza.

"Don't like it?" Logan nodded at her cheese, pepperoni, and sausage slice.

She glanced at him. "I like it fine."

Jake opened his bottle of water. "I heard Mark's prognosis for recovery is pretty good. It'll just take a long time."

"I heard their money is running out." Quinn took another slice of pizza from the box.

"Where'd you hear that?" Jake asked.

"Barrel. He's pretty good friends with Mark. Wish there was something we could do."

Jake pursed his lips. "Let's talk to Wyatt and Virgil. And probably Barrel. There has to be a way to help Mark through this."

"Could be as simple as a few of us helping out a few hours each week. I'd be willing to help," Logan said.

Sam nodded. "If it goes that way, you can count me in."

"I'll mention your idea to Wyatt," Jake said. "Changing the subject. Has anyone heard more about the person who set the fire?"

Quinn shook his head. "You'd be in the best position to know, Jake."

"Only what Laurel Maddox told Aiden." Jake swiped his hands down his already dirty jeans. "Not much more we can do tonight. Might as well head home."

Logan caught Sam's attention. "Are you still up for heading to town?"

"Not for dinner. But music and dancing would be fun after the week we've had."

"Give me thirty minutes, and I'll pick you up."

"Make that forty-five."

Logan gave her a mock salute. "Forty-five it is."

Chapter Eight

Sam didn't expect much at Dulcy's. Not that she anticipated anything other than some improvement in her mood. The fire and thoughts of Mark and Amanda's situation weighed heavy on her mind.

The band was good, the crowd large and enthusiastic. Enough so, as the minutes passed, her energy improved, as did her mood. When the band took a break, a pretty, middle-aged woman with long brown hair, walked onto the stage. Picking up a microphone, she scanned the crowd.

"Anyone up for a line dance lesson?"

The crowd cheered and clapped. The noise continued until the floor was full of women and a few men, all taking spots facing the stage. Sam joined the first line.

Logan watched from their table. His thoughts turned to the fire, then to Sam. Their friendship continued to grow as they spent more time together.

He'd viewed her as another of the ranch hands. A person to share their free time without any expectations. Over his time being around Sam, the expectations shifted in a way he wasn't prepared to define.

Logan didn't do girlfriends. Not since being dumped in high school by a girl he'd come to care about. They'd been an item during his junior and senior years. He'd expected the relationship to continue when both attended community college. Her thoughts had been different.

One and done. He almost laughed at the cheesy expression. Silly or not, the phrase defined his life since high school.

Sam had him rethinking his aversion to another relationship. Watching her line dance, he couldn't be certain if the change included Sam or some other woman.

It had to be someone else, he scoffed. Sam was great, but not the woman of his dreams. Smart, funny, a hard worker, and pretty. Why not Sam? His brows furrowed as he wondered if not Sam, who was the woman of his dreams?

When the music ended, she walked back to their table, picking up her bottle of water for a long swallow.

"That was just what I needed." She took a smaller sip.

"Yeah?" His voice came out weak and distant.

"Great song, fun dance. I'll probably never do it again, but, oh well..." Sam shrugged, the smile still brightening her face.

The band returned, choosing a fast two-step. Logan stood, holding out his ha   's dance."

Miguel Hobson sat at the bar on the other side of the room. He drank a second beer as he watched the action on the dance floor and at various tables. Making a game of guessing what the customers did for a living helped to pass the time. Something he had a great deal of since losing his last job.

One person had caught his interest. A pretty woman with short black hair, dark eyes, and a complexion consistent with those who worked outdoors. She'd marched onto the dance floor, taking a spot in the front row for the line dance lesson.

Afterward, she threaded her way between tables to one occupied by a handsome young man who sat alone. Miguel wondered at the man's name, how he'd met the woman, and how close was their friendship.

When the man stood, holding out his hand, the woman didn't hesitate to thread her fingers with his. The couple danced well, as if they'd been together a long time.

Miguel knew that wasn't the case.

Finished with his beer, he motioned the bartender for a third drink. After all, he had a short walk to the room he rented. He grinned at the thought of the tiny room in an old building. Though in good condition and clean, his fingers almost touched the walls when he extended his arms.

Miguel overlooked the room's shortcomings. The tiny room fit his miniscule budget. As an added advantage, he could pay by the day instead of signing a lease.

"Are you here by yourself?" An average looking young woman, with long red hair and green eyes, nodded toward the empty place beside him.

"Yes."

"Wonderful." She draped her shoulder bag over the back of the bar stool and sat down. When the bartender arrived, she ordered a soft drink. Something Miguel hadn't expected. "I come here for the line dance lessons. My work shift starts at ten at night, so I don't stay long."

Miguel cocked his head to the side. "Where do you work?"

"At the hospital. I'm a nurse."

"Hmmm." He returned his attention to the dance floor. "What do you do?"

"I'm a mechanic."

"All cars, or do you specialize?"

He looked at her, his eyes narrowed in irritation. "All types of cars." His clipped response got through to the woman, who picked up her soda and turned away.

Miguel shifted in his seat in an attempt to find the couple on the dance floor. He spotted the man first, standing by a table, talking to the couple seated there. Panic whipped through him when he couldn't see the woman. Seconds passed before he saw her returning from the hall where the restrooms were located.

Miguel let out a long breath, chastising himself for overreacting. Then again, he'd traveled a long way to find her. When the time was right, he'd approach the woman, and smile while he ruined

"What is going on here?" Sam watched as the two dogs played near the corral by the destroyed barn. Both belonged to the Kelman Ranch, yet it wasn't unusual for them to end up at Whistle Rock.

Duke had been rescued from a pack of wolves by Jake. Rowdy, younger and still somewhat of a pup, had been given to Abbie by Quinn. The two had become fast friends. You rarely spotted one without the other being nearby.

"They followed me down the road." Logan knelt down, scratching Duke behind his ear before rubbing Rowdy's belly. "I thought I'd lost them."

"Yet here they are."

"They're the most predictable dogs I know." Logan straightened.

"What are you doing here today?"

"I volunteered to help with rebuilding the barn. Jake is going to talk to Wyatt and Virgil about helping Mark and Amanda Swanson."

Sam touched his arm. "If you hear we're clear to help out, let me know. I want to be in on that."

"Will do. What are you doing today?"

"We have a new group of guests arriving this afternoon. Oh, and one guest is staying for a third week."

"Laurel Maddox," Logan said.

"How did you know?"

"No great mystery. Between you and Daisy, everyone at the ranch knows she's been here two weeks already and is looking to buy a building downtown."

"Has she made an offer?"

"Not that I've heard. I would've expected you to know. Woman to woman stuff and all that."

Sam laughed. "Woman to woman stuff? That's good. I'll have to tell Daisy. And no, I haven't spoken to Laurel. It is a truly spectacular building inside. Outside," she shrugged, "needs a little TLC."

"Which building is it?" Logan continued to watch the dogs running around them.

"It was a café and soda shop for a long time. Daisy remembers it from high school. It's between the bank and a building leasing space to professionals."

Logan snapped his fingers. "I know it. A cream and pink exterior, and lots of carved wood inside."

"That's it. The paint is so faded it doesn't even look like pink anymore. I hope she's able to buy it. Laurel would be a great addition to the area."

"She sure would."

Sam took a step closer to him. "What do you mean?"

He scratched the back of his neck. "Well, she's a real nice lady, smart, motivated, and beautiful." Logan waved at Brady Blackwolf, who'd just exited the large barn. "I'm sure glad the small barn burned and not the biggest one."

Sam nodded, her mind still on his description of Laurel. She wondered why his words bothered her so much.

"Hey, Logan. Sam." Brady chuckled as Rowdy and Duke ran around and between them. "Are you two going to work on the barn?"

"Virgil hasn't told me," Sam answered. "This week's guests start arriving in a couple hours."

"That's why I'm here," Logan said. "You?"

"I'll be working with you. Virgil just let me know." Brady looked over his shoulder at the burnt building. "Something bothers me, though."

"What's that?" Sam asked.

"We don't know who started the fire, or why. What's stopping the person from torching it again once we rebuild?"

Sam pursed her lips. "I suppose if nothing happens, we'll know it was a guest who left yesterday or this morning."

Brady shook his head. "Only if they left the ranch. They could've taken a room at a hotel."

Logan looked between Sam and Brady. "Well, nothing we can do now. The decision's been made to rebuild now, so that's what we'll do."

"I suppose so." Brady walked away, the question of who started the fire still bothering him.

"His point is valid, Logan. Maybe Wyatt should post someone at night to keep watch."

"I heard he and Virgil have people watching."

Sam's eyes widened. "I hadn't heard. I wonder who?"

"No idea, but I'll ask Virgil when I see him. I'd better join Brady so we can get started. Duke and Rowdy will be fine on their own. See you later."

"Sure. See you later." Sam watched him walk off. She didn't like the strange feeling at his leaving. It was almost as if...

Sam shook her head. "Nope. We are not going there," she whispered.

Hearing a vehicle approaching, she looked up to see a battered blue truck parked in the open lot. A man got out, settled a black Stetson on his head, then turned to face her.

Sam's stomach churned as her chest constricted in a painful pinch. "It can't be him."

Yet she knew it was. The one man she never wanted to see again. The same man who'd almost destroyed her life.

Miguel Hobson. Her no good, rotten ex-husband.

Chapter Nine

Sam paced as she waited for the new guests to arrive on Sunday afternoon. As with the previous weeks, this one was full. Every guest cabin would be occupied, resulting in a busy week of activities. Just the way Sam liked it.

Unfortunately, her mind wasn't on the upcoming week. Her thoughts were with the man in the lodge, meeting with Wyatt and Virgil.

After all this time, why would Miguel Hobson track her down? Sam knew the chances of him showing up without knowing she worked at Whistle Rock were zero. First, the man had never been much of a cowboy. Second, as far as she'd heard, he still lived in Oklahoma and worked as a mechanic. Third, her mother would've called her right away if she knew he'd moved out of town.

"The miscreant had slipped out of town during the night. The same as any weasel."

"Are you talking to yourself, Sam?"

She whirled around to face Logan. "Me? Talking to myself? Never."

"I'm pretty sure you were. And you were talking in full sentences."

She lowered her voice. "Was I that loud?"

"I don't believe anyone heard you but me." He patted her shoulder. "Tell me about your miscreant."

"Ugh. You did hear me."

"Told you I did. Now, who's the weasel?"

"It's not a discussion I want to have out here. Honestly, I don't ever want to have the conversation."

"Curiouser and curiouser." He winked at her. "You know that just piques my interest even more."

"Well, it will have to stay piqued until after work when we can talk alone."

Logan grew serious. "If you're in danger, you'd let me know. Right?"

She relaxed. "Thanks, Logan. But I'm not in danger. I promise to tell you later. All right?"

"As long as you let me know if whatever it is should be dealt with sooner. Agreed?"

"I agree. Now, get back to building the barn."

"While you continue pacing." Logan didn't wait for a reply before he jogged toward the barn.

Sam assisted a family of four to their cabin, showing them the amenities and handing out a schedule of each day's events. The entire time, she continued to watch the lodge. The instant Miguel left, she'd find Wyatt or Virgil. One or both would know why he'd visited the ranch.

Leaving their cabin, she spotted Miguel on the front porch of the lodge. Wyatt and Virgil were with him, listening as he spoke in his usual animated manner. Her stomach soured at the sight.

She thought back on all the times he'd tried to explain away his bad behavior. Good-looking with an abundance of charm, he'd become used to getting out of trouble with slick excuses.

Sam rushed to the large barn, ducking inside before Miguel could spot her.

She didn't try to peek out at him. Busying herself with repairing tack would be a better use of her time than constantly peering out to see if he'd left.

The first piece in the repair box was a frayed throatlatch. Underneath, she found a torn curb strap. She started with it. Her plan had been to spend fifteen or twenty minutes fixing the leather. Forty-five minutes passed as she focused on her work. Finishing, she appraised her work, satisfied the strap would last a long time. Checking the time on her phone, she jumped up.

The guests would be entering the lodge for their welcome reception and orientation. She'd be working with children from twelve to seventeen. Her favorite group.

Dashing across the open area to the lodge, she rushed inside. Halting at Wyatt's strong voice, she moved behind the adults to the table where ten children stood around. Sam looked at each one, and would've laughed if it weren't for Wyatt's welcoming speech.

They ranged in size from under five feet to over six. She guessed the oldest were two boys who had to be six-two and close to a hundred and eighty pounds. Sam opened her phone to type a message into her note app. *Discuss age groups for those seventeen and under with Virgil.*

Waiting until Wyatt concluded, she introduced herself. "I've been a ranch hand here for a while."

A girl of around twelve raised her hand. "What do you do?"

"The short answer is that I do everything the men do with a few exceptions." She ignored the older boys who snickered. "Tomorrow, I'll show you examples of what ranch hands do. Anyone who is interested may try out a few of them."

"I want to ride a bucking bronc," one of the older boys said, laughing.

"I'll see what I can do. If you don't have an activities list for the week, pick one up on the table before you leave. There will be a trail ride on Wednesday. You don't want to miss it. I'm pretty certain you'll find the week is full of things you'll enjoy."

"What's going on tonight?" A girl of about fifteen looked eager and ready to learn.

"After dinner, a couple of the boys will demonstrate calf roping. When they're finished, you'll have a chance to try it with a calf roping dummy."

An older boy scoffed. "One of those lame heads stuck in a bale of hay?"

"Ours are better than most. It's not as easy as you think. Later in the week, you'll be able to rope a moving calf."

"One that runs around?"

"Yep. That'll be on Friday. Well, it looks like the meeting is breaking up. I hope to see you after dinner in the small arena."

Sam watched her group walk toward the adults. Which at Whistle Rock meant eighteen years old and up. She headed straight for Virgil.

"We really have to change the age categories. It's real hard to excite boys of seventeen when the others in the group are twelve and thirteen." She glanced across the room and froze. Leaning against a counter was Miguel Hobson.

"You're right. Let's talk at breakfast."

She glanced back at Virgil. "Great. I'll see you then." He started to turn when she snagged his arm. "Did that man over there come to see you?"

Virgil followed her gaze. "Me and Wyatt. He's looking for a job."

"You don't want him here."

Virgil's eyes widened at the vehemence in her voice. "You know him?"

"I do. Trust me. He'll bring nothing but trouble to this ranch." Before she said something she couldn't take back, Sam walked out the back

"Do you know where Sam is?" Logan had stopped next to a group of several ranch hands, including Barrel and Brady.

"She's with Virgil," Barrel answered. "They're on a trail ride with the younger guests." Brady and the rest of the ranch hands dispersed, leaving Logan and Barrel alone.

"Do you expect them soon?"

Barrel checked his watch. "Within the next thirty minutes. Do you want to stick around? Or I could pass along a message."

Logan rubbed the back of his neck. "Let her know I'll be at Mark Swanson's place. She wanted to ride over with me, but I don't want him to think we aren't coming."

"No problem. This your day, huh?"

Logan nodded. "Have you already been there?"

Barrel bent down to pick up a rock, tossing it toward the side of the barn. "Went there yesterday. There's a lot to be done. Virgil's only allocated two hours at a time to help Mark and Amanda out. Honestly, it would take several ranch hands a week of full-time hours to get his ranch close to where it needs to be."

"I figured as much." Logan peered out into the distance. "That may be them."

Barrel nodded. "Yep. I believe it is."

Logan waited until the group had dismounted before walking toward Sam. Maybe it was his imagination, but she turned away when her gaze landed on him. His pace slowed.

"Hey, Sam."

Turning back, she closed the distance between them. "How are you?"

"I'm good. Do you still want a ride to the Swanson place?"

She winced. "Geez, I forgot about us going. Just let me grab a couple things and I'll meet you at your truck."

"Sure thing."

He watched as she dashed toward her cabin. Sam didn't forget much, especially something as important as helping a neighbor.

Sam washed her face longer than necessary. The cool water helped to draw her thoughts away from Miguel. She'd thought about him throughout the trail ride, sometimes missing questions from the guests, and forgetting about her commitment to work at the Swanson ranch.

She grabbed a towel, soaking up the rivulets of water dripping down her face. Sam didn't have to look in the mirror to know lines of worry were already appearing. It had happened throughout her short relationship with Miguel. Her stomach would sour, discomfort visible on her face.

Walking to a chair, she sat down, closing her eyes. After all this time, why was he here? She knew it wasn't a coincidence. Miguel always had a reason for everything, and those reasons were never good. She wondered what disaster he had planned this time.

"Hey, Sam. Are you coming?"

Jumping up, she tossed the towel aside. "Yeah, I'm coming."

"I'll be at the truck," Logan shouted through the open door. "I have plenty of water."

"Okay. Thanks." Lifting her small purse from a hook,

she slung it over a shoulder.

Logan had the truck running by the time she slid onto the passenger seat. She remained quiet as he pulled onto the road which led to the highway.

"Barrel told me it's going to take a lot more than a couple hours for a few days to set things right at the Swanson place."

She nodded. "He told me the same. I'm sure whatever we're able to do will help. I don't mind putting in more than the two hours the Bonners are paying us. I'll gladly work a few more if it will make a difference."

"The biggest decision is what to do, and in what order. Barrel made it sound like the work is almost overwhelming."

Forcing herself out of the depression Miguel's appearance had triggered, she looked at Logan. "Hey. We thrive on overwhelming odds. The bigger the challenge the sweeter the reward. Right?"

Logan shot her a look before bursting out in deep laughter. Turning off the highway, they continued on a country road before taking a long dirt drive toward the Swanson Ranch. He glanced at her before slowing for a deep rut.

"Are you going to tell me what's bothering you?"

"I don't know what you mean."

"Come on, Sam. We both know something's eating at you. If it's none of my business, tell me and I'll back off."

Staring out the window, her jaw clamped tight. It wasn't his business, yet it would be so nice to talk it through with someone.

"Sorry I brought it up."

"No. You're right. I'm just not sure I'm ready to talk about it."

"I won't push you, Sam. If you want to talk, I'm a good listener." He stopped the truck outside a weathered barn in obvious need of repair. "Here we are." Logan opened his door.

"Wait a minute." Her voice was small, almost unrecognizable. "A man came to the ranch today." She paused to gather her thoughts. "He spoke with someone in the lodge."

"You don't know who he spoke with?"

"I believe it was Wyatt or Virgil."

"Why would it matter? There are always people coming to Whistle Rock to speak with someone."

"This time, it was different." She swallowed, gathering her thoughts.

"Why do you care who it was?"

"There's this thing. Back in my past."

Another minute passed before Logan spoke. "Okay. What's *this thing*?"

"I saw the man's face. I recognized him. His name is Miguel. He isn't a good man."

"And you know he isn't good because..."

She let out a deep, unsteady breath. "Because I was married to him."

Chapter Ten

Logan's throat tightened. He didn't know how to respond to Sam's announcement. Married? He'd never thought about Sam having a serious relationship. Logan didn't know why it bothered him. Maybe because they'd become friends.

Yeah, he thought. That had to be the reason.

"You were married?"

She felt her face heat. "Yes. Does that seem ridiculous?"

"Not really. I'd just never thought about it. Guess I figured you would've mentioned it by now."

A slow nod was her only response.

"You're sure your ex-husband was who you saw go into the lodge?"

"Positive. Believe me, I'll never forget Miguel's face."

"Why'd you divorce?"

"It's a short, but complicated story, Logan. Not something I want to go into now." Opening her door, she got out, walking straight toward the barn.

"Hey, Sam!"

She turned to see Amanda standing on the front porch. Smiling, she headed toward the house.

"It's good to see you, Sam."

"Sorry we couldn't get here earlier."

"Are you kidding? Mark and I are glad to have whatever

help you can give us. Would you and Logan like to come inside for coffee before starting?"

Logan joined them. "We'll pass on that for now, Amanda. Let us know what you want done and we'll get at it."

"Right now, we're concentrating on repairs to the barn. The way it is now, we doubt it'll last another Wyoming winter. I'd say start on the stalls." She handed Logan a box. "That's new hardware. Mark and I will be out in a few minutes."

"No rush. Sam and I will get started." He gave a two-finger mock salute before walking toward the barn with Sam.

The instant they entered the cavernous space, he turned to face her. "Our conversation isn't over yet, Sam. Be prepared to answer some questions on our way back to Whistle Rock."

Over two hours later, and after coffee with Mark and Amanda, they drove back to the ranch. Logan fought the urge to ask the promised questions. Looking at the total exhaustion on Sam's face, he decided to put his curiosity off until another time.

"Do you feel like stopping for dinner?" When she didn't answer, he glanced over to see Sam slouched in her seat, fast asleep.

Instead of waking her, he found himself wondering

about the man she'd married. While working together to repair a horse stall, she'd confided Miguel's last name was Hobson.

"Miguel Hobson. What do you have planned?" Logan whispered to himself, careful not to disturb her.

She'd mentioned the man meeting with Wyatt and Virgil. He was certain they'd tell Sam what was discussed with her ex if she asked. Something held her back. He wondered what.

Parking near the lodge, he sat for a moment, watching her. With her face serene, she appeared to be no more than eighteen years old. Logan hated interrupting her sleep but had little choice.

Virgil agreed to allow the ranch hands to volunteer at the Swanson ranch as long as the time didn't interfere with their regular work. He worked for his brother at the Kelman Ranch, but Sam worked for Virgil. While Quinn might cut Logan some slack, he had no idea what Virgil would do.

Walking around to the passenger side, he opened the door, pressing a hand against her shoulder so she wouldn't roll out. He chuckled when she didn't stir.

"Sam." He repeated her name again. This time, his voice penetrated, and she woke with a start.

Sitting up, she looked around. "Sorry." She failed to stifle a huge yawn. "Guess I fell asleep."

"You conked out within minutes of us leaving the Swanson Ranch."

She shoved him out of the way, sliding out of the truck. "I'm starving. Bet you are, too."

"I could eat."

"Great. We'll raid the kitchen. There must be leftovers just waiting for us."

He followed behind as she led the way to the kitchen's back door. The lights were still on inside, spotlighting a large bowl of fruit set in the center of the large working island. The place where all the real work went on in the kitchen. To the left of the bowl was a covered dish with the remainder of what appeared to be carrot cake.

Walking past the island, Sam opened the refrigerator. Within minutes, Sam had the fixings for beef and ham sandwiches. Between the two of them, Logan and Sam put together three large sandwiches. Two for Logan, and the third for Sam.

Preferring to stand at the island, they spoke little as they devoured their late meals. When only breadcrumbs remained, Sam cut two large slices of cake. Between hefty bites of cake, they spoke about the Swanson Ranch and all that needed to be done.

"I just don't see how Mark and Amanda will be able to continue without hiring help. We can do some, but not enough to keep them afloat." Sam picked up her plate, washing it in the sink.

"Jake said something over dinner the other night. He didn't come right out and say it, but it seems the Bonners are putting together a plan so the Swansons can keep their ranch."

Sam's brows raised at the news. "Any idea what the plan is?"

"Nope. Jake didn't share any specifics."

"Maybe because the Bonners haven't agreed on all the details." Sam stared out the kitchen window toward the barn. "You've heard how Anson can be."

"Do you mean how obstinate?"

"I'm not certain it's obstinance." She paused a moment. "He always seems to throw obstacles in the way of anything his sons put together."

"Guess it's his right. He's the one who grew Whistle Rock into one of western Wyoming's largest and most profitable outfits."

"True."

"In the little time I've been at the Kelman Ranch, all the ideas Wyatt and Virgil back get approved."

Sam nodded. "Eventually, and most times with a lot of pushback from Anson."

"Seems Anson will grumble about anything out of the ordinary. It's just the way he is. As long as they keep pushing a plan for the Swansons, it's almost guaranteed to happen."

Logan took his plate to the sink, setting it on the counter after washing and drying it. "I should get going."

Sam walked outside with him. It was the first time she'd ever felt a sense of unease around Logan.

"Guess I'll see you around, Sam." He didn't wait for her to respond before turning toward his truck.

Watching him drive off, she felt a strange heaviness in her chest. She couldn't recall the last time the sensation gripped her. Sam wrestled with the combination of longing and emptiness on the short walk to her cabin.

Early the following morning, Barrel, Jimmy, Kenny, and Owen led a large group of guests on a trail ride. An active hot springs near the far northwest corner had become a favorite destination of those visiting the ranch.

Gage and Virgil controlled the activities each week. Both were flexible. If enough guests wanted to make the trip to the springs twice during their stay, they'd add it to the schedule.

They were organizing another ranch rodeo. This one would be different from the others in that it would take place at the Kelman Ranch.

Jake still recalled the words of Seth Magnus, the previous owner who'd passed away not long after selling the ranch. Knowing Jake's plans, he suggested a ranch rodeo would be an excellent way to introduce Wagyu beef to the guests at Whistle Rock Ranch. Wyatt agreed and held firm about holding the rodeo at Jake's ranch when Anson insisted it should take place at their ranch.

As the foreman of the Kelman Ranch, Quinn took on the responsibility of organizing the rodeo. Logan had become his go-to guy in the process, doing a remarkable job of rounding up competitors from neighboring ranches. It was scheduled for late that afternoon, after the guests returned from their trip to the hot springs.

Sam, in her desire to help the Swansons, had almost forgotten her offer to assist with the rodeo. It had been Logan's text message earlier that morning that jogged her memory. Rounding up Brady, and two more Whistle Rock ranch hands who'd volunteered to compete, she drove them to Jake's ranch after lunch.

Climbing out of her truck, she spotted Logan supervising several men as they set up props for each event. A few men worked in two corrals while several others assembled spectator stands. She'd heard Jake say they expected close to sixty people to watch the events.

The additional Whistle Rock men talked with Logan before joining the others. From what she could see, the set up wouldn't take much longer.

"Hey, Sam!"

She turned to see Quinn jog toward her. "Hey, yourself. Appears everything is ready for the spectators."

"We're real close. Logan's done a great job. Thanks for bringing more men. We're going to need them when the guests arrive."

"He asked me to keep the competitors on schedule. Are all the people who signed up to compete still coming?"

"As far as I know. Well, except for Amanda Swanson. Mark's taken a turn for the worse. They're at the hospital."

Her stomach dropped at the news. "Logan and I were there yesterday. He seemed tired, but fine."

Quinn shrugged. "All I got was a brief voice message. I called Beth. She's going to spread the news at Whistle Rock.

I know several of the ranch hands have been helping them out."

"This isn't good news. Do you mind if I try calling Amanda before checking in with Logan?"

"Not at all. I don't know if they have family in the area, but I'm sure any support would be welcome. I'm going to check on the stock we're using for the events."

Pulling out her phone, she called Amanda. She answered on the fourth ring.

"Amanda, it's Sam. How's Mark doing?"

A long silence was followed by what Sam thought was a soft sob. "Not good. The doctors don't know what's causing his pain. They're still doing tests."

"What kind of pain?"

"He woke up about four this morning. That's not unusual. Except he could barely move. Everything hurt. His back, legs, arms. I try to keep him from overdoing it, but he's so stubborn. I got him in the truck and came here about five. Mark griped the whole way here. Thank goodness the doctor in emergency supported my decision."

"Who's with him?"

"Mason Nagle was the first to see him when I got Mark inside. Gabe Montez joined them. They're still in the emergency room. Gabe said he'll come out as soon as they have news. Waiting is killing me."

"Is anyone with you?"

A long sigh came across the phone. "Neither of us have family close by. I've called his parents in Idaho. They're waiting to hear more before making a decision to drive down."

"I have a few things to take care of, then I'll join you."

"You don't have to do that, Sam. I know the ranch rodeo is taking place today."

"Quinn and Logan will understand. Same with Virgil. Waiting is easier when you've got someone with you."

"Thanks, Sam."

"I'll be there within the hour."

"Wait. Doc Montez just came out. Hold on a minute."

Several minutes passed before Gabe Montez's voice came on the line. "Sam?"

"Yeah, I'm here. How's Mark?"

"Well...the news is bad."

"How bad?"

"Real bad, Sam. Hold a second." He returned to the call a minute later. "Amanda's not able to talk right now, but she gave me permission to tell you."

"Don't drag this out, Gabe. What's happening?"

"He suffered a cardiac infarction not long after I joined Doctor Nagle. Mark is stabilized, but...well. Look...if possible, Amanda needs someone to sit with her."

"Tell her I'm on my way."

Chapter Eleven

Sam sprinted from the truck into the emergency waiting area. Her gaze swept the crowded room. Mothers held children, an elderly couple gripped each other's hand, a man wearing a leather jacket sat stoically in a corner. Amanda was absent.

The door to the emergency room opened as she reached the desk where a woman of about fifty looked up. Before she could ask, Amanda appeared in the doorway. Empty eyes roamed the room, landing on Sam. The sight of her broke whatever kept Amanda together. On a sob, she lurched forward.

Rushing forward, Sam caught her. Neither spoke as they made their way to a couple of empty seats. Amanda sat rigid, hands clasped tight in her lap. Eyes vacant, Sam waited for her to explain. Instead, Doctor Gabe Montez appeared before them, dropping to a crouch. He covered Amanda's hands with his.

"I am so sorry. We did all we could, but...it wasn't enough."

A painful knot lodged in Sam's throat. She wanted to ask what Gabe meant, choosing to remain silent. To her surprise, Amanda spoke next.

"I...uh, don't know what...to do." Her broken voice was a lance to Sam's chest.

Gabe opened his mouth to respond when the outside doors opened. Margie, Lily, and Daisy, holding a sleeping Reece, came straight toward them. Standing, he stood before the matriarch of Whistle Rock Ranch. His former employer, the woman who'd convinced Anson to sponsor Gabe through medical school, searched his eyes.

"How is he, Gabe?"

He shook his head. "He's gone, Margie."

"Gone? What do you mean?"

"Mark suffered two massive heart attacks. We just couldn't save him." He looked down at Amanda, who remained seated next to Sam. "I am so sorry."

Margie looked at Daisy and Lily before sitting on a chair on the other side of Amanda. Placing an arm over the younger woman's shoulders, she drew her close.

"I know you're not sure what to do next. What you must remember is you have a lot of friends who love you. These friends will get you through this."

Amanda turned her head to meet Margie's determined gaze. "He's gone."

"I know, sweetheart."

"I don't understand."

"No one does."

"What do I do now?"

A tear rolled down Sam's face as she listened to them. She couldn't quite wrap her head around what had happened.

Margie squeezed Amanda to her. "You'll come with us. Together, we'll take care of everything."

The ranch rodeo was long over by the time Sam parked in front of Jake's house. Sitting behind the wheel, the events of the afternoon replayed in her head. Nothing made sense. Last night, Mark had been joking and laughing with her and Logan. Now, the once gregarious, gentle man was gone.

She didn't know how much time passed between parking and a soft tap on the window. Turning her head, she met Logan's gaze.

Sam knew Lily had made several calls, leaving messages when no one answered. Looking into Logan's eyes, she knew he'd heard the news.

She could hear Rowdy, Abigail's young dog, whining, then barking for attention. The Bernedoodle puppy had been a gift from Quinn to his future wife. He now lived at the Kelman place, and along with Jake's dog, Duke, roamed freely between home and Whistle Rock.

Logan opened the door, catching Sam in his arms as she rolled out. Feet landing on the ground, she looked up at him.

"Mark..." The one word caused another tear to fall.

Logan tightened his hold on her. "I know."

Resting her head against his chest, she sucked in a shaky breath. "I don't know why this had hit me so hard. I didn't really know him."

"We just spent the evening working with him and Amanda. Less than twenty-four hours later, he's gone. Don't dissect it, Sam. You're entitled to mourn him."

"Amanda is a mess. Margie is staying with her until Mark's parents arrive from Idaho."

"Come inside. Beth saved dinner for you."

"I'll stay for a bit, but I'm not hungry."

Rowdy whined again as he rubbed against her leg. Reaching down, she stroked his head.

Without another word, Logan guided them up the steps and into the house where Jake and Beth lived. The couple, plus Quinn and Abigail, sat at the dining room table. Other than nods to acknowledge her presence, only Beth spoke.

"Are you hungry, Sam?"

"No. Coffee would be good, though." She headed toward the kitchen, stopping when Beth held up her hand. "I'll get it. Cream and sugar are on the table."

Logan pulled out a chair for her. As another wave of sadness washed over her, Sam didn't think too much about the welcome gesture.

"Is someone with Amanda?" Jake asked.

"Margie is staying with her. Mark's parents should arrive by morning." Sam used both hands to cup the mug of coffee Beth placed before her. The gesture calmed her.

Rowdy stood, moving across the room to Sam. He rubbed against her leg, prompting her to run a hand over the dog's head and back. Another gesture which comforted her.

Sipping the coffee, she met Logan's gaze. The intensity of his emerald green eyes caught her off guard. He was as handsome as his older half-brother, Quinn. Squeezing her eyes shut, she gave a quick shake of her head.

"Are you all right, Sam?" Abigail leaned toward her, worry clear in the woman's eyes.

"Just tired. It's been a long day."

"And not a particularly good one," Quinn added.

"So true." Finishing the coffee, Sam stood. "I'm going to head home. Thanks for the coffee."

Logan met her at the door. "I'll drive you back."

"I don't need you to drive me."

"I know. Still, it's going to happen."

She looked past him to the others. The looks on their faces told her they sided with Logan.

"I'm too tired to argue."

"Good."

"Want me to follow you down?" Quinn asked.

He shook his head. "Thanks, but I'll walk back."

Opening the truck's passenger door, he motioned her inside. For a woman used to long days of manual work, he watched Sam fumble with the seatbelt, too tired to latch it.

"Don't worry about it. We'll be at your place in five minutes."

When he parked at Whistle Rock, the sight of a group of ranch hands caught his attention. They sat around a fire ring, along with a few guests.

He walked Sam to the door of her cabin, setting a hand on her shoulder. "Get some rest. My guess is tomorrow's going to be another long day."

"You're right. Goodnight, Logan."

"Sam."

When the door closed, he debated a moment before joining the ranch hands at the fire. Lifting his chin at the others, he lowered himself onto a large log.

"You heard about Mark Swanson?" Barrel asked.

"I did. Sam was at the hospital with Amanda."

"Geez," Barrel said. "We heard it was a heart attack."

"Two of them." Logan explained what Sam told him. "Margie is staying with Amanda."

Barrel gave a slow nod. "Word got to the guests after they returned from the ranch rodeo. Made for a somber dinner. Most went right back to their cabins afterward."

"Understandable. It'll hang over everyone for a while." Logan closed his eyes, letting the warmth of the fire seep into his tired bones.

Sam drank her first cup of coffee of the day, staring out of the cabin's front window. She'd made the decision to wait on calling Amanda until Margie returned from the Swansons. She wanted to connect with her friend, though she wasn't inclined to drive over, not with her in-laws there.

Seeing the ranch hands and guests leave the lodge after breakfast, she grabbed her hat and gloves. A solid day of work would help move thoughts of Mark to the back of her mind. At least, she hoped it would.

She was thankful for another beautiful Wyoming day. Checking the list of activities, a small smile broke across her face. Gage planned a trip to the lake for kayaking and another of his nature talks. She loved both. Getting away for a few hours sounded perfect.

Margie returned as Sam walked toward the barn. Changing direction, she met her on the front steps of the lodge.

"How's she doing?"

Margie sighed. "As you'd expect. Didn't sleep and won't eat. Her in-laws arrived about four this morning. The family has a lot of decisions to make."

"Such as what to do with the ranch?"

"That's one of many."

She looked Margie over, seeing lines of weariness around her eyes and mouth. "You look beat, and I've got to get to my chores." She turned to leave.

"Sam? Give Amanda a call later today. I don't think she has many friends around here."

"I'll do that."

Jake stopped Sam on the way to the barn. "Are you still up for a trip to the lake?"

"I'm looking forward to it."

"Good. Barrel and two other hands have loaded the kayaks. They've already left for the lake. A few more guests signed up to go, so we'll need a total of fifteen horses. Brady has started tacking them up."

"I'll help the kid out. Anything else?"

"I'd appreciate it if you could get the lunches from Beth and pack them. Drinks, too."

"I'm on it, Jake. See you when we get back."

Chapter Twelve

Logan watched Miguel Hobson through the truck's front window. Quinn had sent him to pick up the ranch's order at the feed store. Arriving at the counter, the clerk had been speaking to a man applying for a job.

"Be right with you, Logan."

"No hurry, Ed. Take your time."

Ed turned back to the applicant. "Well, Miguel. I'll give this to our manager. He'll call you if he's interested." Ed lifted the form. "How do you pronounce your last name?"

"Hobson, just like it's spelled."

Hearing the last name, Logan had raised a hand. "Hey, Ed. I have to pick up something else. I'll be back in a few."

"Sure thing, Logan. I'm here till closing."

Logan had rushed to his truck, where he now sat, waiting for Miguel to get into one of the other vehicles.

It took Miguel another fifteen minutes to leave the store. Logan wasn't sure what to do, other than follow him. Maybe he'd learn where Miguel lived. It might ease Sam's mind to know his address and that he'd been looking for work.

Following him out of the parking lot, he kept a couple cars between them as Miguel wound through the town. He made one other stop. The hardware store had a large sign in the window stating they were hiring. Logan guessed Miguel had applied.

When he left, Logan pulled right behind him. Another five minutes passed before Miguel pulled into a lot at the south end of town. It was an old building known for short-term room rentals. Logan drove on, made a U-turn, and continued back to the feed store.

Packing the order into the back of his truck took longer than expected. When Ed began talking about Miguel, Logan relaxed and listened.

"You just don't know about people."

"What do you mean, Ed?"

"Do you remember the man who was here earlier?"

"Sure."

"Miguel Hobson. The manager made a few calls. Found out Miguel skipped town without paying rent the last two places he lived. If I'd skipped, you can bet I wouldn't have listed those places on my application." Chuckling, Ed shook his head before jumping out the back of Logan's truck.

"I'm guessing the manager isn't going to hire him." Logan was pretty certain what Ed told him was confidential, but he let it go.

"Heck no. He'll have to find a job somewhere else."

Logan drove back home while thinking over Ed's last comment. From his perspective, it had been well-phrased. Miguel needed to find work somewhere else...and in another town.

"He's staying at the rooms for rent place? You're sure about that?" Sam's eyes had grown wide at Logan's news.

"I followed him there. He's applying around town for a job." He told her about Miguel's application at the feed store. "He can cross that place off his list."

"He never was any good at paying rent. Paying for anything, really."

They sat on the tailgate of his truck that evening, sharing a thermos of coffee. "You never told me why you left him."

Sam cracked a tiny smile. "Being a bum isn't a good enough reason?"

Logan didn't answer, choosing to take another sip of the coffee Beth had made. When the silence stretched, Sam stared into her cup and sighed.

"We were too young, and I was too foolish to get married. I thought I knew all about life. Turned out, I didn't know anything." She swallowed another sip of coffee.

Logan continued his silence, waiting for Sam to talk herself out.

"It's such a cliché," she scoffed. "I found out he was cheating. When I called him on it, he emptied our bank account and left town. Funny. It didn't matter to me that Miguel left. Without rent money, I had to go home and face my parents. That was the hardest part." Setting down her cup, she stared up at the clear night sky. "I've never seen as many stars as here in Wyoming. Anyway, I heard Miguel did the same thing to another woman in Nebraska, then again in Colorado. I don't know if all that is true, though.

What I do know is some people never change, and Miguel is one of them."

Reaching out, Logan took her hand in his. They sat that way until the coffee ran out.

The graveside service for Mark Swanson drew a large crowd. Several people from Whistle Rock Ranch attended. Sam rode with Logan, neither speaking during the short ride.

She scanned the crowd, noting the vacant looks on many faces, as if they still couldn't believe Mark was gone. Amanda sat next to her in-laws, looking pale and tired. Sam doubted she'd gotten more than a few hours' sleep since her husband had passed.

The minister did a fine job, his message upbeat with antidotes about Mark from a young boy until his death. As a woman who rarely cried, Sam found she had to work hard not to cry.

She could sense Logan tense beside her, assuming his reaction had to do with the minister's message...until she followed his gaze. Her jaw tightened. The first thought was the man standing across from them didn't belong here.

Anger built at the sight of Miguel Hobson.

He stared back, the familiar smirk appearing. She wanted to yell at him, insist he leave. And not just the memorial service. Sam wanted him to leave Brilliance, and all of Riverdale County.

Miguel continued to watch her. She felt her body buzz at the prospect of facing off with him.

"Don't do anything foolish, Sam."

Her head whipped to look at Logan. His features were set, hard and unyielding. Except for his eyes. They were soft with understanding.

Biting her lower lip, she gave a slow nod. She had no intention of causing Amanda more pain by interrupting the service to confront her ex. Sam felt Logan's hot breath when he bent, speaking close to her ear.

"We'll take care of this after the service."

A sharp nod indicated her understanding. She told herself not to worry about what would happen when Logan confronted Miguel. Her ex had always preferred to settle disputes with loud arguments which often turned physical. She didn't want to see Logan get drawn into anything with Miguel.

When the service ended, she gripped Logan's arm. "Let's forget talking to Miguel."

His gaze narrowed on her. "Are you sure?"

"Definitely. I know Miguel well enough to be concerned about what could happen. Now isn't the place or the time."

"All right."

They made it to his truck before hearing Sam's name being called. She didn't have to turn around to know who it was.

"Ignore him," she told Logan.

"Sam! Hold up."

She winced. "Ugh. He isn't going to take the hint. Might as well get this over with."

Turning, she didn't feel the need to smile. "Miguel."

He stopped too close to her, his gaze moving over her. "You look great, Sam. The years have been good to you."

"Thanks. You look the same. What are you doing in Brilliance?"

"You never did waste time on small talk. Always right to the point."

"That's me." She glanced at Logan before her gaze returned to Miguel. "So, why are you here?"

"A job. And I knew you were here."

Crossing her arms, she straightened. "Why would you care where I am?"

"Well, our parting wasn't so great."

"You emptied our savings and left, Miguel. As I recall, you didn't stick around to see my reaction."

He didn't show the tiniest amount of regret. "I was young and didn't always make the best decisions." He looked at Logan, holding out his hand. "I'm Miguel Hobson."

Staring at the outstretched hand, he shook it for a brief moment. "Logan Sawyer."

Sam cleared her throat. "Now that the niceties are over, how long do you intend to stay in Brilliance?"

"There's no timetable. I'll stay until I'm ready to leave."

Sam's stance became even more rigid. "That's fine, Miguel. All I ask is that you leave me alone."

"Might be hard, Sammy."

"Don't call me that."

"You used to like it." The smirk reappeared, making her stomach clench.

"That was a long time ago, Mikey."

This time, it was his turn to wince. Holding up his hands in surrender, he smiled. "You have a point."

"Tell me why it might be hard to leave me alone?"

"I already told you. I came to Brilliance for a job and to see you."

Sam riveted her gaze on him. "What job?"

"I was supposed to be a bartender at the steakhouse in town. The owner assured me he'd hold it until I arrived. He gave it to his nephew instead."

"Then you don't need to stick around here any longer, right?"

Miguel shrugged. "Turns out, I like Brilliance. I'm applying around town for another job. A grocery store showed an interest in hiring me."

She cocked her head. "Too bad for them."

"Come on, Sam. I always worked. It's just most of the jobs were boring."

"So you'd quit."

"Not until I had another job lined up."

"Seems your recollection is different from mine." She shot a look at Logan. His amused expression shouldn't have been a surprise.

"Anyway, the job wasn't the main reason for me being here. I came to see you."

"What on earth for? We've been apart for years."

Miguel stuffed both hands into pockets and stared down at his scuffed boots. "Something came up."

"I don't care about what came up."

"You should, Sam. It involves you."

Her pulse ratcheted up at the same time dread pooled in her chest. "After all this time, what could possibly involve me?"

"Do you remember the divorce papers you sent to me?"

"Of course. You never returned them. The attorney in Oklahoma said I could file anyway. She took care of it."

He looked back down at his boots. "Yeah."

Her brows drew together. "Yeah, what?"

"About her filing. She, uh...never got around to it."

Chapter Thirteen

Sam sucked in a breath, willing herself to stay calm. Miguel had an issue with the truth. He had to be mistaken about the papers. Surely, the attorney would've called her once she discovered the oversight.

"Never filed?" Her voice was even, disguising the turmoil she held inside. "How could that be, Miguel? The attorney would've called me once she learned of the error."

"She didn't know about it until I stopped by her office to get a copy of the final decree."

"Why didn't she call me, or write, or something?"

He looked out into the distance. "I might've told her I planned a visit and would explain everything."

"You've been here how many weeks and you just decided to tell me?" Sam took a step closer to Miguel. "We both know you're up to something. I want to know what it is."

"I have no idea what you're talking about, Sam."

Sam's voice rose on what she knew to be a lie. "Don't try to pull your nonsense on me. I know there's something else going on. Spill it."

"Fine. You want to know what I want. Here it is. I told the attorney not to file."

Logan stood off to the side, ready to intervene if Miguel made a wrong move. He had to admit, Miguel was everything he expected.

Her voice continued to rise. "Why would you do that?"

"Because I want another chance with you."

Sam's mouth opened, then slammed shut as she considered her response. She wanted to sound calm and rational.

"You're out of your mind!" She winced. So much for being calm and rational.

"I still love you. Yes, I made mistakes, but I'm older now. More mature."

She held up both hands, stopping his protest. "If you see your actions in Brilliance as *mature*, then you and I clearly have different definitions of the word."

"I know the best approach would've been to go to you directly and talk this out. But..." He shrugged.

"Instead, you went to, who?" Sam was afraid she already knew.

"I spoke with Wyatt Bonner and Virgil Redstar."

She felt blood rushing to her face as anger roiled through her. "What did you say to them?"

"The truth. I told them I wanted to see my wife."

Surprising both of them, Sam burst into laughter. "You're kidding?"

"No, I'm not."

The laughter turned into a guarded expression. "What did they tell you?"

He scoffed, shoving his hands into his pockets. "Not much. I don't think they believed me."

"So, they sent you on your way?"

"Yeah. They wouldn't confirm you worked for them. It didn't matter. I already knew you did. I decided to stick around and find work."

"Why, Miguel? There's nothing for you here."

"Sure there is. You're here, Sam. Since we're still legally married, I figured we could give it another try."

Her mouth twisted, brows drawing together, causing a deep frown. "I'm going to be real clear with you. There is absolutely no chance we will ever be together again. Besides," she stepped next to Logan, slipping her arm through his, "we're engaged."

Logan stopped himself from revealing the shock he felt. Though his jaw began to drop, he corrected the action, replacing it with a forced smile.

Miguel's head whipped between the two of them as his eyes narrowed. "When did this happen?"

She squeezed Logan's arm. "A few weeks ago."

"Where's the ring?"

"It's being sized." Logan joined the conversation. His answer surprised Miguel.

"You can't get married. She's already married to me."

"A technicality. Sam and I will sort it out with the attorney. We might even be able to expedite it." Logan didn't have a clue what he was talking about, but thought it sounded reasonable.

Sam had stood silent beside him, stunned at how Logan had jumped right into her lie. She felt bad about the subterfuge, just not enough to stop the ruse. If Miguel believed they were planning to marry, he might give up and leave town.

"When is the wedding date? If I'm still here, I'll plan to attend."

So maybe he wouldn't leave, Sam thought. Undeterred, she stepped closer to Logan's side. "Sorry, but I don't envision you on the guest list."

Shrugging, the grin on Miguel's face indicated he was far from giving up. "You never know what will happen."

Sam glanced around, noting they were the last ones to leave. "We have to be somewhere. By the way, Miguel. Why are you even here, at Mark's memorial service?"

"I applied for work at his ranch a few days before he died. He seemed a decent guy, so I decided to stop by."

Something in his voice didn't support his words. Refusing to make an issue of it now, Sam decided to leave.

"We need to get going, Logan."

He offered a sharp nod as his gaze locked on Miguel. "I expect you to leave Sam alone. You and I are going to have problems if you don't. Do you understand?"

Miguel gave a negligent shrug before turning to walk away.

Several seconds passed before Sam realized he hadn't answered Logan's question.

Deputy Aiden Winters knocked on the open door, peering into the cavernous space. "Mrs. Maddox?" Cans of paint were set around the room, with large tarps covering counters and the floor. "Mrs. Maddox?"

"I'm upstairs. Be right down."

He stood in the middle of the space, staring at the stairs. When she came down, he smiled, stifling a chuckle. She wore a white industrial coverall, the hood covering her hair. Sensing his amusement, Laurel held her arms out and grinned back.

"I know. It may be overkill, but I don't have to worry about ruining my clothes. I didn't pack old work clothes when I flew out to the guest ranch." She slid the hood off her head.

"You mean leasing an old building in Brilliance wasn't on the activity list Gage hands out?"

She laughed. "Not even close. How about a tour?"

"That would be great."

"We'll start upstairs. That's where I've been working today."

Aiden walked to the stairs, motioning her to go ahead of him. "I'll follow you."

She led him into the apartment.

He took a quick look around. "This is huge."

"Much bigger than I need. There is one large bedroom, two small ones, and two bathrooms. Plus, a huge storage area. It takes up the same space as the retail area downstairs."

"Are you going to leave it like this?"

"It's doubtful. I spoke to a local contractor about remodeling the space to have three apartments with one bedroom and one bath each. I talked to several people around town, and they all said there isn't much for single people to rent."

"You won't live up here?"

"For a time, I might. My plan is to buy a house after the shop opens. There's a real cute one three blocks from here."

"Are you going to buy it?"

"I'd love to, but I have to sell my house back home first. It's on the market, so we'll see what happens. I'll explain what I'm doing downstairs."

Laurel pointed out where the cut flowers and arrangements would be placed, the section highlighting non-floral gifts, and the soda fountain.

"I guess it's obvious." She felt her face heat. "The counter kind of gives it away."

He grinned at the color creeping up her face. "And the large mirror and shelves on the back wall. What you're doing is quite the undertaking."

"I know it seems that way to most people around here."

Aiden raised his brows. "Which means you have secrets."

She laughed again. "They aren't secrets. It's just no one has asked me."

He pointed to the badge on his shirt. "I have no problem asking questions. What experience have you had?"

"Experiences is more like it. My father was in the Army. I've lived all over the country. In high school, I worked for a burger and soda shop on weekends and full-time in the summer. The owner was great about teaching me the business. He was getting ready to retire and wanted at least one employee to have information about the shop."

She pulled a bottle of water from a back pocket and took a long swallow. "There's water in the cooler behind the counter."

"I'm good, thanks. Did your father buy it?"

"Unfortunately, Dad died not long after I graduated."

"Sorry to hear it."

Laurel shrugged before continuing. "Mom had money from her grandmother, and a smidgeon from the Army. She bought the burger shop. I worked there and managed it when Mom was gone. It was a great experience. When she met a man and remarried, she sold the shop and moved to Florida." She shrugged in a *life happens* gesture. "My degree is in horticulture, so that was what I planned. When I saw this place, it seemed natural to combine the two. Flowers and ice cream. What do you think?"

"I think you, Mrs. Maddox, could do anything you want."

"Please, call me Laurel."

"Virgil said you're a widow. I'm sorry."

She expelled a slow breath. "Yeah. My husband was in the Navy. He was on a, um...assignment, and didn't return. KIA."

Killed in action, Aiden thought. "That's rough."

"He would've loved this place."

A minute passed before Aiden spoke. "I should be getting back to my job."

"You probably didn't stop by for a tour. Did you want to talk to me about the fire at the ranch?"

He nodded. "I wanted to fill you in on what we've learned. The sheriff and I had an idea of who started the fire. When the man left the ranch, he headed home. We notified the local authorities, and they kept watch on him. Within a few days, they caught the man attempting to start a fire near his hometown."

"Well, that's good news. I appreciate you letting me know."

Aiden walked to the front door, his hand hovering over the handle. "No problem." He stood there a moment, then turned back toward her. "I know you're busy, but how about dinner some time?"

A slow smile brightened her face. "I do have a lot to do. Still, I do have to eat."

He took a step toward her. "Did I just hear a *yes*?"

"I suppose it is, Deputy."

"Call me Aiden. And I'll contact you to arrange dinner."

Chapter Fourteen

"Heard you and Sam are engaged." Barrel climbed out of his truck in front of the Kelman barn. He reached out a hand, giving it a hard pump when a stunned looking Logan accepted it. "Surprised everyone. Congratulations, man."

It took a moment for him to find his voice. "Uh, thanks. Have you talked to Sam?"

"Sure have. She seemed a little tongue-tied."

"Did she say anything to you?"

Barrel's grin preceded a nod. "Yep. She said, *thanks*. Looked as surprised as you do now."

Clearing his throat, Logan looked past Barrel to see Quinn walking toward them. "How did you find out?"

"Virgil announced it at breakfast. The look on Sam's face..." Barrel barked out a laugh. "I thought she was gonna pass out."

"Any idea how Virgil heard about it?" Relief washed over Logan when Quinn stopped to talk to another ranch hand.

"Virgil didn't say, but I heard flowers and a card were left in the kitchen before dawn. It was addressed to Wyatt, so Beth took them to him when she arrived. Guess the card wasn't signed. Wyatt has no idea who left them. Why? You aren't getting cold feet already, are you?"

"Me?" He shook his head. "Not at all." *Did feeling as if his stomach was tied in a pulsing knot count as cold feet?*

"Sam's a great gal. Sure would like to find me a gal who knows as much about horses and ranching as she does." He slapped Logan's back. "She's a keeper."

"Yeah."

"I'd better get back. See ya around."

"Right. See ya."

Quinn came up beside him as the truck drove off. "What did Barrel want?"

Logan stared at his boots, ignoring the question as he thought about how to answer.

"Too hard a question for you, little brother?"

Looking up, he pinched the bridge of his nose. "I guess you haven't heard."

"Heard what?"

He told Quinn the full story, concluding with Barrel's visit.

"You're saying you and Sam are engaged, but not engaged?"

"That would be right."

A deep bark of laughter emerged from Quinn's throat. "A counterfeit engagement. Leave it to you to keep things interesting. How long is this going to last?"

"Heck if I know. Until Miguel leaves town."

"Or you two marry." Quinn laughed again.

"That is not going to happen. This is a temporary arrangement to keep Miguel away from Sam."

"Any chance he's the one who left the flowers?"

Removing his hat, Logan ran a hand through his already damp hair. "I wouldn't bet against it. The way he left Sam the first time was downright low. He says he's changed."

"You don't believe it?"

"Not a word. He's slick. Charming one minute and a gutter snake the next."

"And as soon as he's gone, so is the engagement?"

"Totally." He nodded for emphasis. "Absolutely." He nodded again.

"You're sure about that?" Quinn offered a wry grin.

"You bet," Logan answered before seeing the mirth on his brother's face. "Guess I've gotten myself into a mess."

"Not at all. You helped a friend. No one can fault you for that. I do have one question."

"What's that?"

"What are you going to do when Miguel leaves and you realize the engagement isn't fake?"

Quinn's question haunted Logan the rest of the day. He hadn't called Sam, and avoided her text messages. They needed to talk in person, not over the phone.

After a shower and dinner, he drove to Whistle Rock Ranch. Expecting to find Sam in her cabin, he lifted his hand to knock, then dropped it to his side.

Their friendship had taken a bizarre turn, one he never would have foreseen. When he'd gone along with Sam's ruse, he hadn't figured on explaining it to his brother and ranch hands. It was certain most of the townsfolk had already heard, either from Miguel or someone from Whistle Rock Ranch. Pressure built inside his chest. He glanced up when the door drew open.

"Are you intending to stand out there all night?"

A mirthless chuckle escaped. "It occurred to me."

"Bet it did. Come inside so we can talk."

"Any chance you have coffee?"

"A full pot." She held the door wide, allowing Logan to scoot past her.

Neither spoke when she pulled two mugs out of a cupboard, filling each with fresh coffee. "Milk, sugar?"

"Black is good." When she set the cup in front of him, he touched her arm. "Thanks, Sam."

"It's just coffee. We've got more significant issues to talk about."

"Barrel drove to the ranch this morning to congratulate me."

She took a sip of coffee. "Yeah, he told me. I guess he told you how Virgil made the announcement at breakfast. I about lost the little I'd eaten."

"Virgil didn't talk to you first?"

"He did, but I didn't expect him to announce it to everyone."

"What did he say?"

"He showed me the note and flowers. Asked if it was true. I told him it was, but it sure never occurred to me he'd tell everyone." She dropped her head back to stare at the ceiling.

"It'll work out, Sam." The calm in his voice belied the storm in his stomach.

"How? It's already a mess."

"That's what we have to figure out. Do you want to hear what I think?"

"Sure."

"It isn't in Miguel's nature to stay for long. He's a man who's always seeking the next big deal. My guess is he came here to live off your success at the ranch until ready to run again. After he leaves, we'll wait a bit, then announce the engagement is off."

She thought a moment before nodding. "That should work. Broken engagements happen all the time." A wry grin crossed her face. "At least, that's what I've heard."

"Until then, we act as any other engaged couple. You'd know more about how they act than me."

"Not really. Miguel and I were never engaged. We decided to marry, went to the local city hall, and said the vows."

Logan walked to the counter, refilling his cup. "Shouldn't be hard. All we have to do is hold hands and act as if we like each other. Are you going to contact the attorney?"

"I called her this morning. She feels awful about what happened. The papers have been filed, and she's working to get the divorce expedited. She warned me it could still take a few months. All I can do is wait until she gets back to me."

"Months..." Logan blew out.

"Miguel won't stick around. Once he's gone, we'll call off the engagement. Until then, our lives will go on as usual. Are you still all right with this?"

"It's a little late to be asking, Sam."

"Not really. We can call it off now, if that's what you want."

Setting the cup aside, he leaned toward her. "I already agreed to this, well...whatever it is. I'm not backing out now."

Beth and Abigail scrubbed the kitchen until there wasn't a speck of dirt to be seen. The deep cleaning took place once a month, though both women were adamant about working in a clean kitchen.

"How much longer do you plan to work here?" Abigail looked up from cleaning the two large ovens.

"Why? Do you want my job?"

"No offense, but that's not what I want."

"Why not?"

"As much as I enjoy cooking, it isn't what I plan to do the rest of my life." Abigail sprayed cleaner on a cloth, wiping it over the front of the ovens.

"What do you want to do?"

"I've been studying the use of medicinal plants for a while now. There was this holistic clinic close to the cafe where I worked. I'd hang around the place during lunch breaks."

"They didn't mind?"

"It was owned by an older woman. She didn't mind at all."

"Was she a doctor?"

"Not that she ever said. Her husband was until he died. She kept the clinic so she could sell her medicinal creations." Abigail straightened to look at Beth. "They were real popular. She collected the plants and used them to create lotions, soap, creams, and such. Made pretty good money. I found it all real interesting."

"You'd quit here to start your own business?"

"Maybe someday. This is a great place to work, and the Bonners are wonderful. I won't leave anytime soon."

"Margie doesn't think it will take long. Seth Mangus, the previous owner, was already a success by selling his beef to restaurants. Jake took over that business when he bought the ranch. With Quinn's help, he'll expand with Wagyu beef. At some point, Jake and I want to start a family. That's when we'll discuss me leaving."

Abigail rested a hip against the counter. "A little boy, like Daisy and Wyatt's?"

"I'd take several if they're like Reece. He's a real cutie."

"That baby is the only person who can soften up Anson when he's in one of his moods."

"So true," Beth agreed. "It's good to see him so concerned about the baby. He and Margie have watched Reece more than once."

"I've volunteered. So far, Daisy hasn't asked."

"The day will come. Don't doubt it."

They laughed, getting back to work.

Several minutes passed before the door to the living room inched open. The door stood open, though no one appeared.

"Do you need help?" Beth asked.

They heard boots shuffling on the wood floor before the door was thrown wide. Nacho walked into the kitchen, a broad smile on his weathered face.

Chapter Fifteen

"Nacho!" Beth hurried to him, wrapping her arms around him for a hug. He smiled even through his grumbling about her action. Pulling back, her gaze swept over him. "You look wonderful. At least twenty years younger."

"You have learned to lie while I was gone, eh, Chica?"

"Not at all. You look rested. What are you doing here?"

"It is a long story, and a sad one. I will not discuss it today. Who is this?" He nodded at Abigail.

"This is my assistant, Abigail Sawyer. Abbie, this is Nacho."

"I've heard so much about you, Mr. Nacho. I'm glad I finally got the chance to meet you."

"Just Nacho, Chica."

Abigail moved to the coffee station. "Would you like coffee?"

He shook his head. "No coffee. Not unless you have tequila and cream?"

Beth smiled at him. "You know we don't keep liquor in the kitchen. Except for special occasions. And I do believe this is one of them." She nodded at Abigail to make him a cup. "Do you have bags with you?"

"They are in my car."

Beth's eyes grew wide. "You're driving?"

"I have done many things since leaving here. You will be surprised."

"I'm already surprised. Are you hungry?"

"No. I will sit down, though." He walked to the table and chairs in the corner, lowering himself on a deep sigh. "I drove too far today."

Beth sat down across from him. "Have you seen any of the Bonners, or Virgil?"

"Not yet. The lodge is quiet." He glanced around as if assessing what was once his kitchen.

"You know that Wyatt and Daisy had a baby boy not long ago?"

"Yes. They mailed a picture to me."

"They're in town for a doctor's visit. Anson and Margie went with them. They plan to eat dinner at the steakhouse. Virgil is around here somewhere. You're going to be here for a while, right?"

"Sí, Chica."

"Excellent. Virgil will know if there's a cabin available. If not, one of the apartments in the back is open."

"The apartment is fine."

"Great. If you give me the keys, I'll get your bags."

He placed a hand over his heart, giving her an aggrieved stare. "No, Chica. I am still able to carry my own things. First, I will search for Virgil."

Nacho nodded at Abigail before leaving through the kitchen door.

"He wasn't what I expected."

124

Beth agreed. "He looks much better than when he left here to live with his brother. I wonder what happened to him."

"Nacho?"

"His brother. He wasn't well, which contributed to Nacho's decision to leave the ranch. I hope his brother recovered."

"But you're thinking the opposite."

Beth nodded. "Yes, I am."

"What if he returned to get his job back?"

"Don't worry about it, Abbie. If he did, then the Bonners will make room for him. It's the way they are."

"You're sure?"

Beth couldn't miss the worry in Abigail's voice. "Absolutely." In truth, she wasn't sure at all. "Let's get dinner started."

"You've been avoiding me."

Logan turned around to face Sam. The smile he saw didn't fool him. Her assessment had been right.

"Sorry, Sam. I've been swamped."

"Not swamped enough you couldn't have sent a text." It wasn't a question.

He set aside the tool in his hand. "You're right. I don't have an excuse. Except..." He rubbed the back of his neck.

"Except, what?"

"Guess I'm still trying to figure out how to act. Or what to say when asked about the engagement."

"I thought we already agreed on a plan."

"We decided what to do once Miguel leaves town." He shrugged. "But you're right, Sam. I needed a few days to figure out what to do next."

"That's easy. We talk to each other and spend time together. We do it often enough for word to get back to Miguel that this is real. We're the only ones who know it's not."

Seconds ticked by before Logan responded. Checking his watch, a grin formed. "It's Friday. Are you up for pizza, Sam?"

"I'd love pizza."

"Drive back to Whistle Rock and I'll pick you up. Give me fifteen to clean up, and we'll be on our way."

"I'll be waiting."

Sam climbed into her truck, heading back home. She didn't have to guess where they'd go. There were two places to get good pizza in Brilliance. One was takeout and delivery only. The second had inside tables, a few arcade games, and offered beer as well as soda and water. The ranch baseball team frequented the place the previous summer. Guest ranch duties and other projects this year made it impossible to field a team. Maybe next year.

Parking, her gaze landed on a figure she recognized. Her smile was immediate. Climbing out, she headed straight for Virgil and Nacho.

"Good to see you." She held out her hand for him to shake. "Are you visiting or back for good?"

Accepting her hand, he shot a look at Virgil. "This one is sharp."

"All the women are," Virgil answered.

"I may stay a while, Chica. We will see."

She wondered what would happen to Beth and Abigail if he stayed, deciding to keep the question to herself. It wasn't her business, and what would be would be.

Nacho looked at Virgil. "The girls said I could stay in the empty apartment behind the kitchen."

"Fine with me." Virgil shuffled his boot on the hard ground. "Wyatt shouldn't have a problem with you staying there." He glanced at her. It took a few seconds before she got the message. He wanted to speak with Nacho alone.

"I'm waiting for Logan to pick me up. I'd better grab a jacket before he arrives. Welcome back, Nacho."

She thought about his surprise arrival and how it could affect both ranches. Sam knew Beth and Abigail needed their jobs. Their incomes helped support Jake Kelman's ranch until he could gain traction with his new venture of offering Wagyu beef to restaurants.

The money from current sales of Angus beef were steady. Predictable is what Beth had called those sales. Those clients, plus what Jake and she made at Whistle Rock, kept their ranch going.

Grabbing a lightweight jacket from a hook in her cabin, she stepped back outside, yelping when she ran into a hard wall of muscle. Raising her gaze, she groaned.

"Miguel. What are you doing here?" Placing both palms on his chest, she shoved him away.

"We need to talk. Alone."

"No, we don't. Nothing you say will interest me. You need to leave." He blocked her when she attempted to move past him. "Get out of my way."

"I'm only asking for a few minutes to talk."

"Our marriage was over long ago." Crossing her arms, she glared up at him. "There is absolutely nothing to talk about."

"I don't believe you are engaged to Logan."

"It doesn't matter what you believe, Miguel. Now, move."

"It would be best if you did what the lady asked." Sam moved to look around Miguel at the same time he whirled to face Logan. "She's made herself clear. Leave and don't return."

Sam noticed Miguel's fingers flexing as if in preparation for a fight. A brawl wasn't acceptable. Not with the ranch hosting a large group of visitors. Moving quickly, she inserted herself between the men.

"Enough of this. Logan is right, you need to leave. We have nothing to discuss. If you have something to say, put it in a letter."

Miguel threw back his head and laughed. "You want me to write a letter?"

"That's right. I'll read it when there's time."

"You'll throw it away."

"I said I'll read it, and I will." Sam already knew Miguel would never take the time to write her. He talked, or fought, to get his point across. She'd witnessed him write a letter or peck out an email. "You need to leave. Did you drive here?"

"I walked."

Her eyes grew wide. "All the way from town?"

"It isn't so far. Two, maybe three, miles."

Logan stepped closer, locking his gaze on Miguel. "You should start back now. Before Virgil or Wyatt catch sight of you."

Tearing his attention away from Logan, he shifted to face Samantha. "It is important we talk."

"Fine. Write me a letter. If I think it's important enough to meet, I'll let you know." Sam didn't say another word before walking toward Logan's truck.

"You don't love her."

Logan thought it a ridiculous comment. "I think we both know *you're* the man who didn't love her. Sam has a bright future here at Whistle Rock Ranch. She's surrounded by people who care about her. I can't think of a single reason any man would want to cheat her out of a good life."

"A life with you?" Miguel smirked.

"Yes. With me."

Chapter Sixteen

"The shop is really coming along, Laurel." Aiden walked around the huge space which she'd separated into smaller areas with the skillful use of new walls and pieces of furniture. The wood floors had been refinished, the walls painted, and new lighting fixtures hung on the walls. "Will the soda fountain open at the same time as the flower shop?"

"That's the plan. I've had two high schoolers and a recently divorced young woman apply for work." She stopped arranging product on a shelf and smiled. "I haven't even advertised for help yet."

"There aren't too many places offering work in Brilliance. Most additional jobs happen in late spring or early summer. They're filled just before the summer visitors arrive. Your shop will cater to locals *and* visitors."

"Which means, I'll be able to offer work all year long."

Aiden nodded. "That's right. It will be a big deal to those who truly need work."

Laurel stopped what she was doing to look at him. "You know a lot about Brilliance."

"Not really. I do understand small towns and the difficulty finding work." He walked behind the soda counter, bending to take a peek at the shelves. "When will your supplies arrive?"

"As early as this afternoon. Realistically, tomorrow or the following day. I learned a long time ago not to plan around deliveries."

"What about flowers and food?"

"Not until the day before we open. The freezer will arrive in a few days. The refrigerated display for flowers should be here soon. I won't schedule the grand opening until the shop is perfect."

"I figured as much."

Shifting toward him, her mouth twisted into a grin. "Being picky has always been a blessing and a curse. My late husband used to tease me about being a perfectionist. It took a long time to complete our living room because I couldn't find exactly what was in my head. It was finished days before he, um...left." Swallowing the painful lump in her throat, she opened another box.

Aiden couldn't miss the ache in her voice when she talked about her late husband. He waited to see if she continued. When she returned to her work, he stepped closer.

"Can I make a suggestion?"

Confusion showed in her eyes. "Of course."

"I'm off duty. Have dinner with me. Afterward, we'll come back together, and I'll help you with whatever needs to be done."

"You don't have to do that."

He chuckled. "I know. We both have to eat. Might as well do it together."

She thought a moment. "All right. But you don't have to come back here."

"It's like this. At home, there's nothing but a stack of mail to open, emails to read, and a television I haven't set up. Helping you would be a good way to spend some time."

Glancing down at her less than chic clothes, she grinned. "I don't have a change of clothes."

"No problem. Brilliance is full of casual restaurants."

"Mexican?"

"Works for me."

Laurel hesitated a few more seconds before nodding. "Well then, let me wash my hands and lock up."

His grin mirrored hers. "Have at it. I'll be waiting out front."

"Two chicken enchiladas, one carnitas taco, one beef taco, one chicken tamale, rice, and beans. Oh, and a large iced tea." Sam closed her menu, handing it to the waitress who stared down at her.

"All of this is for you?" The young woman let her gaze move over what she'd written.

"Sure is. I'm hungry."

The waitress's attention moved to Logan. "Sir?"

"The same, except I would like two chicken tamales."

"Okaaayy." She turned to leave, then whirled back around. "I'll get those drinks right out."

Logan gave her a nod. "Thank you." When she was out of earshot, he rested his arms on the table. "What are we going to do about Miguel?"

"He's like a starving dog with a bone. As long as we don't change our story, he'll get bored and leave." Sam grabbed a corn chip from a basket, broke off a piece, and popped it into her mouth.

"Weeks? Months?"

Sam waited to answer until the waitress set down their drinks and left. "I have no idea."

Logan picked up a large corn chip, dipped it into the salsa, and took a bite. "This is great." He chewed, swallowed, and picked up another chip. "We can't wait months, Sam. Let me rephrase that. We don't want this to drag on for months."

"I know. Other than actually getting married, I have no idea what to do but wait." She glanced up to see Logan's feature go slack as the color drained from his face. Laughing wasn't appropriate, yet that's what she did.

"I'm not suggesting we get married, Logan. Jeez, I'm not that crazy." Lifting her glass, she took a long swallow of iced tea.

"I know you aren't crazy. Just don't say things like that." He looked away, his gaze landing on Aiden Winters and a woman he'd seen somewhere before. "Who's the woman with Deputy Winters?"

Sam turned, recognizing her. "That's Laurel Maddox. She's the lady who bought the building downtown. I should go say hello. Why don't you come with me?"

Sliding the chair back, he followed Sam across the room. As they approached, Aiden spotted them and stood. He held out his hand to them.

"Laurel, you know Sam and Logan."

Laurel nodded. "Sam was with me when I first saw the building. Why don't you join us?"

"We don't want to intrude," Logan said.

"Nonsense," Laurel said. "Sit down."

Sam looked to Logan, who nodded. "I'll let the waitress know and get our drinks," he said before crossing toward the kitchen.

Sam took a chair next to Laurel. "How is the shop coming along?"

"It's getting there."

"You should stop by and see it, Sam. Laurel's done a great job."

"Thanks, Aiden. He stopped by to see it before we came here. There's still a great deal to do."

Sam thought of her schedule, her mind going to Mark and Amanda Swanson, and how they no longer needed her help. Her mood soured for a moment before she forced a smile.

"I'd be glad to help. Logan might also have some free time."

"That's generous of you, Sam. I'll be at breakfast tomorrow. Can we talk about it then?"

"Sure can." Seeing Logan approach, she felt her face heat. The immediate response disturbed her.

Aiden waited until Logan sat down to speak. "I hear congratulations are in order."

His mind blanked for an instant, but he recovered. Reaching over, he snagged Sam's hand. "Thanks, Aiden."

"What did I miss?" Laurel asked.

"Sam and Logan are engaged."

"What?" She fixed her gaze on Sam. "That's wonderful news. Congratulations."

"Where's the ring?" Aiden nodded toward Sam's left hand.

"We're going to pick one out this weekend. Right, Sam?"

"Um...yes. This weekend."

Their food arrived at the same time. Sam stared down at what had been so appealing a bit ago. Thinking about an engagement ring, the wonderful Mexican food didn't seem as attractive.

Sam worked alongside Brady and Owen the following morning, tacking up horses for a trail ride to the hot springs. Gage planned a different route for this group of guests, lengthening the outing by half an hour.

Tightening the cinch on one horse, she moved to the next, her thoughts on the previous night. She and Logan had shared meals several times since he'd arrived in Brilliance. Not once had she felt uncomfortable about being with him.

Last night felt different, as if they were a real couple. It was an uncommon sensation of belonging which alarmed her. She'd avoided relationships since her marriage to Miguel. He'd soured her for anything more than basic friendship.

She'd found herself staring at Logan several times as they ate. Not quick glances, but longer examinations of his strong features. She wondered what it would be like to actually be his fiancée.

As soon as Sam realized the direction of her thoughts, she'd tear her gaze away, chastising herself for the ridiculous, romantic notions. She wasn't a romantic. Hadn't been since the demise of her marriage.

The problem was she couldn't deny her unwelcome attraction to Logan. She liked him, enjoyed his company, felt a sense of loss when their evenings ended. Nobody had to tell her the feelings were one-sided.

She was older than him, after all. Sam had seen the looks younger women shot him at Dulcy's. What surprised her was how he'd never returned their interest. Logan was content with a burger, a beer, and listening to the band. Once in a while, he'd grab her hand for a dance. Most times, he was fine watching other couples or the line dancers.

He was the most uncomplicated man she'd ever known.

"You going on the ride, Sam?"

So lost in thought, she'd startled at Brady's voice. "Um...no. I'll be staying behind to set up the afternoon activities. Most of the women are going to Daisy's jewelry making class. I'll be helping her." She laughed. "I don't know a thing about jewelry."

"Maybe you'll be watching Reece."

Her jaw dropped. "I'm no better with babies. Although, he is one beautiful boy."

Brady lowered his voice, as if not wanting anyone else to hear. "I helped Wyatt with baby duty a week ago. Easiest kid you ever saw." His brows rose as his smile widened. "Hey. This time next year, I might be helping you and Logan with baby duty."

Chapter Seventeen

"That's great news, Benny. I'll let Quinn know. See you in a few days." Logan ended the call, already walking toward the four-wheeler parked several yards away.

His brother had been waiting for Benny's call. The news Logan carried would be better than Quinn could imagine.

The last message he'd received had his brother working with a few of the ranch hands near the western property line. They were moving the herd, but he didn't know where.

Driving in the direction he expected to find them, he groaned when the four-wheeler sputtered and stalled. He first checked the gas tank. Finding it almost full, the carburetor was next. As expected, it was clean. Logan went through the checklist in his head, unable to identify the problem.

Hands on hips, he looked around. There was nothing to do except head back for the other four-wheeler. It would take him half an hour to walk back to the equipment barn. The reality was Quinn would hear the good news as soon as Logan could get it to him.

He ran as far as he could in his barn boots. Removing them, Logan ran the rest of the way. Reaching the building where Jake kept the equipment, he checked the remaining four-wheeler with care. As with the other one, he saw nothing that caused a red flag.

Climbing on, he started the engine. It sounded fine. Driving outside, he came to an abrupt stop.

Smoke billowed from the direction of Whistle Rock Ranch. Leaving the four-wheeler behind, he got into his truck, navigating the short, winding road in less than a minute.

His mind didn't want to accept what was right before him. The barn he'd helped rebuild was on fire, as was the hay stacked beside it.

"But they arrested the arsonist." Logan punched out the words as he exited the truck, running toward the water supply.

Jake had told him and Quinn most of the Whistle Rock hands would be with the guests on a long ride to the hot springs. It became clear who'd been left behind when he looked around, spotting Nacho, Anson, Wyatt, Beth, and Sam manning the hoses.

"Logan!" He whirled around to face Wyatt.

"What can I do?"

"Spell my father."

Nodding, he spotted Anson fighting to control one of the oversized water hoses. Running to him, he placed his hands alongside Anson's.

"I'll take it for a bit."

The elder Bonner didn't object, taking several steps back as he gasped for air. The sight worried Logan.

"Wyatt!" Catching his attention, Logan nodded toward Anson. Wyatt understood and headed toward his father.

Logan concentrated on the water hose. It was larger than normal, but not as large as those used by firefighters. Still, it was easier to hold it in both hands. He directed the powerful spray at the interior of the barn.

Unlike the previous fire, this one felt hotter, the blaze ferocious. Two other hoses, one at the opposite end of the barn and the other on the northern side, were manned by Barrel and Jake.

A bright light to his right caught Logan's attention. His stomach plummeted. The fire had jumped to the outside of a nearby cabin.

"Jake!" Logan gripped the hose with his left hand while pointing toward the cabin with his right.

Jake responded in an instant, dragging his hose toward the cabin. Virgil ran to him, both yelling at each other to be heard over the noise of the fire. Jake shifted, turning the direction of the spray toward a cabin several feet away.

Meanwhile, Virgil organized a bucket brigade which concentrated on the first cabin while Jake continued to water down the second. Logan knew it was a preventive action meant to save the other structure.

Sirens blared in the distance. A firetruck came to an abrupt stop near the burning barn. Several men jumped from the rig, preparing to take over the fight.

A sheriff's department SUV stopped behind the rig. Aiden Winters stepped out, already scanning the scene with a disgusted look.

Logan handed over the hose to one of the firefighters, stepped away, and spotted Sam with a group of guests. They were crowded together next to the lodge. Some watched the urgent activities to stop the fire while others carried on animated conversations.

Taking several steps toward them, Logan stopped at his name being called. Jake came up beside him.

"The fire captain wants us to move the guests farther away. Can you notify Sam?"

"On my way." Logan ran the short distance, stopping beside her. "We need to move the guests."

"Where to?"

He glanced around, pointing to the front of the lodge. "How about there?"

"That'll work. I can get the guests relocated if you have other things to do."

"I'm good for now. Let's get everyone out of the way."

No one objected to Sam explaining what they needed to do. The heat had risen to an uncomfortable level, encouraging them to move farther away. When finished, Logan and Sam stood next to each other.

"I thought they'd arrested the person who started the last fire," Sam said, her features marked with confusion.

"That's what I heard. Maybe this isn't arson."

"Do you really believe that?"

Logan shook his head. "No."

Sam gave a slow nod of agreement as she watched the newly rebuilt barn disintegrate. "We installed the last of the hardware a few days ago. Now this." Her jaw tightened. "Someone must have a grudge against the Bonners."

"Or someone else at the ranch. Hard to know what goes on in the mind of an arsonist."

"I just can't think of anyone who'd do this." Sam crossed her arms, anger building as helplessness raced through her.

Spotting Aiden make his way toward them, Logan held out his hand. "Deputy."

Clasping the hand, Aiden nodded at Sam and the others. "Logan."

"Thought they caught the guy," Logan said.

"We all thought so. Appears not. I'll need to talk to everyone." He glanced at what he assumed were the guests. They'd huddled together, some staring, others talking. A different group than was at the ranch for the first fire. "Is Laurel Maddox still here?"

Sam shook her head. "She moved into an apartment above the flower shop. Laurel said it was easier for her to get stuff done than driving back and forth each day."

Aiden nodded. "Makes sense. I need to start interviewing your guests. Were any of them here during the last fire?"

"No. Well, except for Laurel." Sam answered without turning her attention away from the activities to stop the fire. "Let me know if you need my help with anything."

"Will do." Aiden moved to the closest group of guests, introducing himself while extracting a small notebook and pen from a pocket.

Sam moved closer to Logan, lowering her voice. "It has to be someone who's never been a guest at the ranch."

"I was thinking the same. Have you noticed anyone from town lurking around?"

She gave a slow shake of her head. "No. I can't believe someone started the fire in daylight with several of us around." Sam looked at Logan. "I've been outside all morning and didn't notice anyone who shouldn't be here."

"Have you considered it might be one of the ranch hands?"

She glanced around as a sigh escaped. "I'm trying not to."

"Could be, Sam."

"I know, but who? Everyone has been here a while. I'm one of the last people the Bonners hired." She rubbed her temples. "I just can't see a ranch hand doing this. Every one of them is a person I'd trust with my life."

"You're sure about that?"

"Absolutely. What about one of the men from Jake's ranch?"

"I don't know any of them well enough to say. Two of them worked for Seth Magnus before he sold the place to Jake. The others are younger and used to moving about. They'll stay a year or two someplace, then find something else. I guess it's possible one of them set the fires, but..." Logan thought a moment before shaking his head. "I just can't understand what they'd have to gain. It would be a huge risk with no payoff."

Before Sam could respond, Aiden left the guests he'd been interviewing and joined them. "Nothing from them. I

143

wanted to double check with you two. Either of you see anything suspicious?"

"No," each answered.

"Did anyone show up you didn't recognize?"

Sam shot a look at Logan. "He was working at the Kelman Ranch until he saw the smoke and drove over. I didn't see anyone who didn't belong here."

"The same answer as everyone else," Aiden mumbled more to himself than to Logan and Sam. He looked at the fire. "I wonder if our arsonist is someone battling the flames."

"They're mostly the firefighters at this point. You aren't implying it's one of them, are you?" Sam asked.

"I have to consider all the possibilities. Brady Blackwolf is a volunteer firefighter, right?"

"He is, but he's with the rest of the guests on a trip south of town."

Aiden glanced at her. "Any other volunteers?"

"Not that I know about." She turned away, attempting to get a better view of how the men were doing in their efforts to squelch the fire. Her heart sank. The fire had jumped to an equipment barn. "Oh, no."

Both Logan and Aiden followed her gaze, then jumped when the structure exploded.

Chapter Eighteen

"Gasoline." Sam took a step forward, coming to an abrupt stop when Logan grabbed her arm.

"Leave it to the professionals." He loosened his grip but didn't let go. Instead, he moved his hand down to thread his fingers with hers. She didn't pull away.

"How much gasoline is there?" Aiden asked, staring as three four-wheelers were engulfed in flames.

"Not much. Most of the extra gasoline is in a metal shed over there." She pointed toward another barn and the small structure next to it.

As they watched, Jake and Barrel ran to the shed. Unlocking it, they ducked inside, coming out with five-gallon jugs in each of their hands. After setting them down a good distance away, they returned to retrieve four more.

"That should be all of it." Sam's attention moved back to the equipment shed, stomach plummeting at the extent of the damage. Her fingers tightened on Logan's.

Added to losing the barn for a second time, she felt anger swell within her toward whoever set the fire. She whirled around to face Aiden, but he wasn't there. Looking toward the lodge, she saw him talking to Wyatt and Anson.

"I wonder what Aiden is thinking?"

Logan looked down at her. "I doubt he has much to go on. The fire investigator will have to come out again."

"I heard there's a new one. A female from some big city back east. Seems the original investigator took a job in Montana. His last assignment was when our barn burned down the first time."

"Back east, huh? Wonder what got her out this way?"

She shrugged. "Who knows? You know how city women are."

He gave a slow shake of his head. "Not really."

"They all want to meet a cowboy. I'm sure she'll want to talk to you about the fire."

"Not me." He squeezed her hand. "You saw more than me. She can talk to you."

"You're not afraid of city women, are you?"

"Me? Not at all. I'm just not interested." He looked down at their joined hands. "This fake fiancée thing is all I can handle right now."

A flash of disappointment crossed her face before Sam pulled her hand from his. "I'd better see if I can do anything to help the guests. See you around, Logan." She dashed off before he could respond.

"Dumb, dumb, dumb." Sam chanted the words under her breath as she hurried toward the guests. For a few minutes, she'd fooled herself into believing Logan was holding her hand because he wanted to, and not because of the roles they were playing.

What bothered her most was the disappointment she felt at realizing why he'd threaded his fingers through hers. For a few minutes, she almost believed Logan had feelings for her beyond those of a friend.

The notion seemed ridiculous now. At least she figured it out before making a complete fool of herself.

She joined the guests who hadn't taken the field trip with everyone else. The shock of the fire had worn off, and they were talking among themselves. Sam watched long enough to realize the firefighters had the blaze under control. She raised her voice to grab the guests' attention.

"I'm going to check the cabins to make sure it's safe for you to return."

"They'll be pretty smoky," a tall, boney man with a beard and mustache called out.

"Should we move to other cabins?" the woman beside him yelled.

"First, I need to make sure there's no more danger of the fire restarting. Then I'll check each cabin. Jake and Virgil will make decisions about moving you back in." Before anyone else could speak up, Sam jogged away.

She joined Virgil, Jake, Wyatt, Anson, and the fire captain. "What's the situation with the cabins?"

"We still have to check them out," the captain answered. "Just one caught fire, but it's not safe for the guests to enter until we've done a complete walk-through. They'll have to be patient a bit longer."

"Take them inside the lodge," Wyatt said. "The last I knew, Beth and Abbie were preparing food and drinks for everyone."

"All right." She turned toward the back door of the kitchen, stopping when she spotted Logan with Jake beside him. A low groan escaped when Logan smiled at her.

The groan didn't come from her not being happy to see him. Not at all. The reaction came from how her body responded to him. Sam didn't like the way her stomach fluttered or the tightness in her chest whenever he was close. She wanted the automatic response to stop, go back to the way things were before they decided to discourage Miguel by pretending they were engaged. What a mistake that was turning out to be.

He nodded at her without speaking, his attention focused on Jake and what he had to tell Wyatt. The serious expression on both of their faces kept her in place.

Lowering his voice, Jake spoke to Wyatt, Aiden, and the fire captain. Anson stood next to his son. Logan stayed close to Jake, listening. When finished, everyone except Aiden, who made a phone call, and Anson, walked in separate directions.

Curious, she followed Logan. "Hey. Wait up."

He stopped and turned to face her. "Yeah?"

"What's going on?"

Glancing over his shoulder, he lowered his voice. "Barrel told Jake he saw someone near the barn not long before the fire started."

"And?"

"He's real sure the person was a woman."

Sam sat with the guests inside the lodge, snacking on crackers, cheese, spinach and artichoke dip, sliced vegetables, and sandwiches. Most picked at the food. The weary firefighters ate with vigor while swallowing large amounts of water between bites. The sandwiches disappeared within minutes of their arrival.

Sam didn't eat at all, choosing to sip on a glass of iced tea. The details Logan shared didn't sit well with her.

Barrel's description of the arsonist matched Laurel Maddox. Even though he hadn't seen her face, the height, slender body, and blonde hair worn in a ponytail pointed to her. The fact she'd been in town, and a guest at the ranch for the first fire, supported what he saw.

Sam refused to believe the woman she'd come to think of as a friend could be responsible for both fires. Her reasoning was an arsonist would take time to hide their identity. The blonde ponytail, not hidden within a hoodie or hat, was an example.

She'd told Aiden the same before he left to talk with Laurel. It didn't seem to make any difference to the deputy or anyone else. Barrel's statement carried more significance than Sam's doubts.

"How are you doing?" Logan pulled a chair close and sat down.

"All right. Any word from Aiden?"

Logan shook his head. "He'd be notifying the sheriff if he suspected Laurel. Sheriff Dugan might contact Wyatt." He shrugged.

"It's not her," Sam said.

"I don't know much about her," Logan said.

"She's a widow who put a lot of money into a new business. Why would anyone do that if they were planning to burn down the largest ranch in the area?"

"Who knows what goes on in someone else's mind? Miguel is a good example."

Sam looked at him, her brows drawing together. "How so?"

"Why would he track you down after all this time to try for a second chance?"

"I've thought about that a lot." She leaned toward him. "Miguel never worked this hard to do anything. He's basically lazy. Something else is going on, I just don't know what."

"There sure are a lot of strange things going on around here, Sam."

"Our engagement being one of them."

He barked out a laugh, though the look on his face seemed to convey something else.

Logan drove back home later that afternoon, his mind reeling from what he wouldn't allow himself to accept. He knew his clouded brain was mistaken, sending him incorrect signals. There was no chance he wanted the counterfeit engagement to Sam to be...what? Real?

"Not a chance," he muttered to himself while parking the truck.

At twenty-four, he still had plenty of time to get his life in order before meeting a girl he wanted to marry. Ahead of him were nights at Dulcy's, hanging with other ranch hands while watching single women laugh and dance. No way did he want to miss out on those experiences.

Logan had dated little, most of his youth spent concentrating on work and school. His mother had required his help to pay the bills. Life had been complicated.

His and Quinn's father had been the same man. Their mothers different women due to an affair which resulted in Logan's birth. His father did what he could, but Wallace Sawyer wasn't a rich man. Not even close.

Money made at the small ranch he owned had to stretch across a wife and two children. Adding Logan and his mother to the mix made for a slim existence. From the time he became a teenager, he'd worked whatever jobs were offered to help with food, clothing, and medical bills. Dating had been an activity far out of his reach.

Even now, and with his mother still working her job as a law office receptionist, he sent some of his wages to her each month. He didn't ask what she did with the money. It had never mattered to him. Claudia Baker had bet on the wrong man. A married man who got tangled in an affair with no intention of ever leaving his wife.

Logan had made a promise to himself as a teenager. If and when he married, it would be for life, and there'd be no cheating.

Sam had already been married and divorced. She was older by three years. Wyatt and Virgil considered her one of the best ranch hands at Whistle Rock. She had much more experience than Logan. He also suspected she was much smarter than him.

A wan smile tipped up the corners of his mouth. And she was also much better looking. Not beautiful or stunning, but a very attractive woman with a gorgeous smile.

It was a smile which lit up his world every time she aimed it at him.

Chapter Nineteen

Sam parked her truck in front of Laurel's shop, sitting for a few minutes to gather her thoughts. She hadn't called ahead or heard anything on the status of Aiden's meeting with her. A meeting which Sam guessed had turned into an interrogation.

Leaving the truck, she tried the front door, not surprised to find it locked. She cupped her hands to look inside. When she didn't see Laurel, she knocked again, louder this time.

Several minutes ticked by before Laurel appeared. She visibly relaxed when she spotted Sam standing outside.

"Sorry to keep you standing out here." Laurel motioned her inside. "I didn't know who was here until I came downstairs."

"Trying to avoid Aiden?"

Closing and locking the door, Laurel stared at her. "How did you know?"

"I was at the ranch when someone started the fire."

"I see." Laurel moved passed her toward the soda fountain. "Have a seat. What can I get you?"

"You're already set up?" Sam slid onto one of the stools covered in new black vinyl.

"Pretty much. More supplies arrive every day. Plus, I've hired two people. One for thirty hours a week, and the other for twenty. When school starts, he'll cut back to about ten. How about a chocolate shake? I want to test the equipment."

"I'd love to help you test your shake machine." Sam watched as Laurel prepared the ingredients. "Tell me if I'm out of line, but do you feel comfortable telling me what happened with Aiden?"

Securing the container in the blender, Laurel turned it on. Turning around, she leaned against the counter.

"I don't mind. Aiden asked me questions about my stay at the ranch, what I saw when the first arson fire occurred. He wanted to know where I was when the first started." She turned to remove the container from the blender. Grabbing a shake glass, she poured the chocolate confection into it. "Here you go." She handed her a straw.

Removing the paper, Sam slid the straw into the shake, taking a slow sip. "Oh my, this is fabulous. Your machine worked perfectly. What else did Aiden ask?"

"He kept asking the same questions in different ways. It was as close to an interrogation as I've ever had. I know he was doing his job. It's just, he made me feel as if I was the arsonist. I was angry and annoyed by the time he left. I'll never view Aiden the same again."

Sam set down the glass, having already drank half of it. "I think he's a good guy, Laurel. He's in a tough spot."

"I know you're right. It's just..." She shrugged.

"It's just what?"

"I thought Aiden was a friend. Goes to show you how wrong I can be about people. I should never jump to conclusions."

"Don't write him off so quickly. I mean, what was he to do?"

"You should've been here, Sam. It was as if he'd become a different person. He asked questions over and over until I wanted to scream. All he wanted was to get me to break, confess to setting the fires." Laurel grabbed a damp cloth and began to wipe down the counter. "I finally told him to leave. That shook him up enough that he stopped. He did look a little deflated when I pointed to the door. By then, I couldn't stand looking at him. Aiden figured it out and left. Okay, enough about what happened to me. Tell me about you and Logan. I didn't realize the two of you were serious."

Sam wanted to tell Laurel the truth, knowing it would go against the promise she and Logan made. Every person who knew would give Miguel a better chance of learning it was all a ruse. She had to stick with their plan.

"There isn't much to tell. It happened quickly." She forced a smile. "Guess you never know what life will bring."

"Thank you for calling." A slow, resigned sigh slipped through Logan's lips. "I'll wait for your next call and get there as soon as I can." He stared at the phone in his hand, trying to digest the caller's message.

"Are you all right?"

It took him a moment to remember he and Sam were sitting in a booth at the pizza parlor. He'd been telling her a story about one of the ranch hands when his phone vibrated.

"Uh, sorry. What did you say?"

"The call, Logan. Is everything all right?"

Eyes blank, he gave a slow shake of his head. "It was...it was..." He stood, shoving the phone into a pocket before heading outside.

"Logan. Wait." She followed after him, worried about the vacant look and sudden pallor of his face. Getting outside seconds after him, she gripped his arm. "Talk to me."

Licking his lips, he looked away. "It was about my mother."

"What about her?"

"She's, uh...dead."

Spotting a bench, she tugged him toward it. "Sit down and tell me what they said."

Lowering himself, he leaned forward, resting his forearms on his thighs to stare at the ground. "A man from the hospital called. He said I was listed as her emergency contact." He rubbed his palms against his eyes. After a minute, he turned his head to look at Sam. "She had a heart attack. She's g...g...gone." His voice broke as his eyes watered.

Sam wrapped her arms around him, rocking slowly as the tears came. They didn't last long before he sat up, swiping the dampness away with the back of his hand.

"Can I call someone for you?"

"There's no one. I'm it."

"What about Quinn? He could call your father."

"No. Wallace won't care that she's gone."

Sam knew the story, how Logan had come to Brilliance to find his older half-brother. She wasn't sure Wallace Sawyer wouldn't care.

"You're his son. He'll care about you." When he didn't respond, she took his hand in hers. "What can I do for you? Do you want to go back to the ranch?"

"Yeah. I need to get away from here."

"Wait for me in your truck. I'll be right out. And please, let me drive." True to her word, Sam slid behind the wheel five minutes later. He began talking soon after they turned onto the highway.

"The man said she didn't suffer. She was with a friend at dinner when it happened. She was gone before the paramedics could get her to the hospital."

"I know it doesn't mean much, but that's a blessing."

Resting a hand on her jean-clad thigh, he cleared his throat. "It means a great deal, Sam."

They didn't speak again before she parked close to the barn at the Kelman Ranch. "Would you mind if I stay for a while?"

"I'd appreciate the company. I'm waiting for another call from the man at the hospital."

They entered a small cabin behind the main house. It was the original foreman's place before Jake built a new house for Quinn and Abigail. That structure sat next to Logan's cabin.

Logan entered the living room and looked around as if

seeing it for the first time. Sam stood beside him.

"Sit down and I'll make us coffee."

"Thanks, Sam. Just give me a few more minutes and I'll be fine."

She nodded before leaving the room, doubting he'd be fine. She returned from the kitchen a few minutes later with two cups, handing one to Logan. "It's black. Do you want anything in it?"

"Black is good." He took a sip before setting the cup down. "I feel like I should be doing something. Darned if I know what."

"There's not much you can do until the hospital calls back."

"True. They're releasing the body to a local mortuary. The guy I spoke to doesn't know which one." Restless, he stood. "I should pack. I'll have to leave early tomorrow morning."

"I'll speak with Virgil."

"What for?"

"You aren't going alone. I'll go with you."

"I appreciate the offer, Sam. This is something I have to do alone."

"Why is that?"

Logan didn't respond right away. Pacing to the window, he looked out toward Quinn's house. "It's the way I've always done stuff."

A half-smile appeared as his words clarified what she'd been thinking. "That's about to change."

"I'll get the information to Pop, Logan. I'm sure he'll do his best to be there for you." Quinn drew his younger half-brother into a hug. "Can I do anything more for you?"

Logan shook his head. "You've done enough. Thanks for clearing this with Jake." His head bobbed enough to notice. "I'll finish everything up and get back as soon as possible."

"Take whatever time you need. Call if you need anything." Quinn squeezed Logan's shoulder, looking toward where Sam stood on the passenger side of the truck. "Keep me posted."

She nodded before sliding into the truck. Sam offered to drive, but understood when he insisted he needed something to focus on besides his mother.

The drive wasn't far. Less than two hours in the heavy morning traffic. Sam tried to keep a conversation going on topics other than his mother. When Logan answered in short, clipped sentences, she gave up, deciding silence worked fine.

His mother's body had been moved to the funeral home by the time they arrived. Logan hadn't wanted to stop at his mother's. Dealing with her home would come sometime, just not right now.

The woman they met at the funeral home gave Logan several options, none of which he could afford. Partway through the meeting, his phone rang. Seeing his father's name, he excused himself to walk into the hall.

"Hey, Pop."

"Logan. How are you holding up?"

"How you'd expect."

"Quinn said she had a heart attack."

"That's what the man from the hospital said. Guess it was quick, which is good."

"Are you having a service?"

Logan gave a date a few days away. "Seems a little soon, but there are no relatives to notify. And, well...Sam and I have to get back to work."

"I'm glad she's with you. Quinn said you're going to marry that gal."

Logan hesitated a moment. "Seems so."

"I don't want you to worry about anything. I'm driving out for the service."

"You don't have to do that, Pop. I know it would be awkward for you at home."

"Sally wants to come with me."

"Say again."

"Quinn's mom insists on attending the service. When Sally makes up her mind, there's no changing it. I'd appreciate it if you get us a place to stay."

Logan felt unexpected relief at his father's announcement. "Sure, Pop. I'll take care of it."

"And Logan?"

"Yes."

"Don't worry about the cost. I'm paying for whatever you decide."

Chapter Twenty

Claudia's service was short, marked by a few personal details from her life. Logan was mentioned, but the pastor never touched on his father.

Logan held Sam's hand the entire time, his heart full of gratitude toward her, his father, and Sally. Quinn and Abigail showed up as the service started, surprising everyone.

True to his word, Wallace had already spoken to the funeral home representative about the expenses. He refused to discuss his decision with Logan, who insisted on hosting dinner at a local restaurant.

The entire day, Logan didn't get more than a few feet away from Sam. She'd been his rock, a friend he never wanted to disappoint. If he were honest, the woman he'd come to love.

The days before the service had been spent going through Claudia's few belongings. She wasn't a hoarder, which made their work easier than expected. Logan and Sam packed a few items which held special meaning, taking everything else to a local charity. Claudia didn't own her place, so nothing had to be done after packing and cleaning.

A few people from her workplace attended the service. Each stopped to speak with Logan. The last handed him a card with her name and contact information, informing him about a small life insurance policy the company provided all employees. He'd tucked it in a pocket, planning to call her when he returned to the ranch.

A week after leaving, Logan and Sam checked out of their rooms for the drive home. Unlike the trip to Claudia's, the mood had shifted. Logan had come to accept his mother's death, even making a few decisions about his future. The most important being he didn't want their engagement to be fake.

He parked the truck at Whistle Rock Ranch long enough to carry Sam's lone suitcase to her front door. She stood beside him, removing the key from her pocket.

"Thanks, Sam. I don't know how I would've gotten through everything without you."

"You would've done fine."

He shrugged. "Maybe, but that's not the point. I'm glad you were there."

Before Sam knew what was happening, he slid an arm around her to pull her close. A second later, his mouth was on hers. It wasn't a long kiss, but it conveyed much of what Logan wanted to say.

Without another word, he walked back to his truck and drove away.

Sam touched her lips several times, attempting to figure out the meaning of his kiss. Could it have been meant to convey gratitude for accompanying him? Or helping him sort out Claudia's belongings? Maybe just being there during a difficult time.

None of those made sense for that kind of kiss. It was warm and meaningful, with enough heat to get her heart thumping.

If he'd intended for it to mean something, why hadn't he stuck around? That was easy. He didn't know what to say. In truth, she didn't know what to say about the kiss either. Except...wow!

Sam decided to tuck the subject away to bring up later. Preferably when Logan was around.

Changing into her normal work clothes of jeans, a long-sleeved blouse, boots, and hat, she headed outside. Work on the barn had progressed, though not as rapidly as after the first time it had burned down. Spotting Virgil, she waved, waiting as he walked toward her.

"I didn't know you were back."

"Logan just dropped me off."

"How's he doing?"

"Better. It was wonderful that his father, Quinn, and Abigail were there for the service."

"Well, I'm glad you're back."

"What do you want me to do, Virgil?"

"We need someone to work inside the rebuilt barn. The windows are on order, as is the hardware we need for doors, and feeding bins for the stalls. The automatic waterers have been shipped. There's still work that can be done until everything arrives. Check with Barrel."

"Will do." She started to walk off when Virgil called her name.

"You probably don't know the latest."

"Latest?"

"You remember Laurel Maddox?"

"Sure. She's all right, isn't she?"

"She's fine. Someone broke into her shop and trashed the place. I heard the damage was extensive. Daisy said Laurel's working with her insurance company to get the place fixed up."

Sam couldn't quite fathom someone wanting to destroy the shop. "Someone with a grudge against her?" she said out loud.

"Seems strange. The woman's only been around Brilliance a short time. Aiden Winters is investigating."

That must've gone over real well, she thought but didn't say. "I'll call her later. Maybe I can help her clean up. Thanks for letting me know."

"Any leads on who did this?" Sam moved the mop and bucket behind the soda counter.

She'd shown up at the shop an hour earlier. A grateful Laurel had put her right to work vacuuming and mopping the floors.

"None. Deputy Winters has come by a few times to ask more questions, but that's it."

"Is he still asking about the fire?"

164

"Of course. The man is like a bloodhound. He's picked up a scent and won't give it up without the answers he wants. Unfortunately, I don't have any answers."

Sam rinsed out the mop to start again at the far end of the counter. "No other fires around town?"

Laurel stopped what she was doing to look at her. "No. Why do you ask?"

"It just seems odd that there've been two fires at Whistle Rock and none anywhere else. Don't arsonists usually jump around?"

"I have no idea. You should pose the question to Deputy Winters."

"Maybe I will." Sam worked her way to the other end of the counter, rinsed out the mop, and looked around. "What else can I do to help?"

"All that's left is to restock the soda fountain and gifts. Flowers are arriving tomorrow afternoon."

"When is the grand opening?"

"The day after tomorrow."

"I'll stay here tomorrow night."

Laurel stopped what she was doing. "Stay here?"

"Sure. I may ask Logan to stay, also. We don't want anyone messing with your store a second time."

"You don't have to do that, Sam. I'll be here."

"It would be smart to call Deputy Winters, too. He may want to be nearby."

"Absolutely not. I will not ask any favors of that man."

Sam smiled to herself as she understood Laurel's anger at Winters. The deputy had been on his way to becoming important to her, and Sam was certain the reverse was true.

"If it were me, I'd take whatever help was offered."

Laurel crossed her arms. "The deputy hasn't offered."

"He just hasn't thought about it yet. When he hears Logan and I will be here, I'm certain he'll offer." Picking up the bucket in one hand, the mop in the other, Sam headed to the back room.

"Dump the water down the floor drain."

"Will do." Doing as Laurel said, Sam stopped when male voices came from the front.

They were loud, although she couldn't make out what was being said. Setting down the bucket and mop, she walked to the open door and peered out in time to see Miguel shove Logan with both hands.

She ran toward them, not wanting this to get out of control. "Miguel. You need to leave."

Neither man looked at her, their attention focused on each other. When Miguel pushed Logan again, she pulled out her phone, punching in a number. Her voice rose when Logan responded by slugging Miguel in the arm.

"Sheriff? There's a man creating a disturbance at the new flower shop. Yes, the one on the main street, next to the bank. By the way, his name is Miguel Hobson."

Hearing his name, Miguel glared at Sam before stalking to the front door. Shoving it open, he took one last look at her before rushing outside.

Logan watched him go, unaware Sam had come up beside him. Sensing her, he smiled. "You didn't call the sheriff's office, right?"

"No, but Miguel didn't know that. What happened?"

"He followed me inside, shoved me from behind, then slipped in front of me and shoved again."

"You guys didn't argue or anything?"

"We never said a word to each other. The man is crazy, Sam."

"You're right. It took me much too long to realize it when we were married."

"You were married to that man?" Laurel had walked up behind them.

Sam grimaced. "It's a long story. I'll tell you about it sometime. For now, please don't spread it around."

"I won't breathe a word. It was odd, though. He shoved Logan inside from the back, then got in his face and shoved him again."

"Have you ever seen Miguel around the shop before tonight?"

Laurel gave a quick shake of her head. "No. I don't believe I've ever seen him around Brilliance."

Logan kept his gaze on the front windows and entry doors. "I hope he took off. To be safe, you might want to lock up, Laurel." He threaded his fingers through Sam's. "I'm taking Sam to dinner. Why don't you join us?"

"I appreciate the offer, but I don't want to intrude."

"You wouldn't be intruding. We'd love to have you."

She looked down at her work clothes. Before she could object again, Sam spoke.

"I'm in the same situation. We're going somewhere real casual, right, Logan?" She looked up at him.

"Definitely casual."

"Let me at least change my blouse and lock the back door. I'll meet you back here in ten minutes."

"Perfect." Sam squeezed Logan's hand. After Laurel left the room, she turned to face him. "I didn't know we were going to dinner."

"That was my plan when I came looking for you. I didn't know Miguel was hanging around outside."

"Wait. Miguel was outside Laurel's shop?"

"He was. Looking inside. I thought it real strange."

"And creepy." Sam shivered at the image of Miguel peeking inside at her and Laurel.

"I thought the same. That may be why he reacted by pushing me." He lifted their joined hands to kiss her knuckles. "It's hard to see you married to the guy."

She lifted one shoulder. "Young and dumb."

Laurel joined them. "I'm ready. Where are we going?"

Chapter Twenty-One

"Let me read this back to you. One order each of Kung Pao chicken, broccoli beef, orange chicken, and shrimp fried rice." The waitress smiled down at Logan, her interest clear.

"Plus, three sweet and sour soups." Logan smiled back at the cute young woman with auburn curls, green eyes, and a much too bubbly personality for a Chinese restaurant. At least Sam thought so.

"Right. Three soups. Anything else?" The question was for all of them, though her attention continued to lock on Logan.

It would've irritated Sam if he hadn't been holding her hand, squeezing it when the waitress's smile widened.

"Nope. That's it." Logan tightened his hold on Sam's hand.

When the waitress left, the entrance door opened. A lone man walked in and looked around. Without thought, Logan raised his hand in greeting.

"Hey, Aiden. Come and join us."

Laurel's jaw dropped at the same time Sam kicked Logan's leg. He didn't even react. She mouthed *sorry* at Laurel, pasting on a strained smile.

"Good evening." Aiden looked at the booth, noting he'd be sitting next to Laurel. "Are you sure about joining you? I can find a spot somewhere else."

"It's fine," Logan answered. "Laurel, would you mind?"

She shook her head without saying a word. Scooting over to let Aiden sit down, she left as much space between them as possible. Knowing Laurel's opinion of the deputy, Sam felt bad for her.

"We've already ordered." Logan itemized the menu items for him. "I'm sure there'll be enough for you."

"I don't want to eat your food." Aiden waved at the waitress, who came right over. "This will be on my tab, Izzy."

She bestowed the same smile on him as Logan. "The usual spring rolls and shredded pork with garlic sauce?"

"Yes. And hot tea."

"I'll get the order right in and get your tea."

"Thanks, Izzy." He looked over at Laurel, then across the table at Logan and Sam. "I heard about your mother. That must be tough. Sorry, man."

"Thanks. It was sudden. I spoke to her on the phone a few days earlier. She sounded fine. Sam drove over with me." Logan nodded toward her. "We packed and cleaned up the place after the service for Mom." When he didn't continue, Sam jumped in.

"Quinn and Abigail, plus Logan's father and his wife, attended the service for his mother. It was great to have them there."

Logan offered her an appreciative smile. "Anyway, it's done, and life goes on. Right?"

"Yeah, it does," Aiden said, and changed the subject. "How's the store going, Laurel?"

"Fine."

"It's looking great," Sam said.

"There is one issue, Aiden." Logan's voice held concern.

"What's that?"

"Do you know Miguel Hobson?"

"I've heard of him. Why?"

"When I drove up this evening, he was looking through the window at the women." He nodded toward Sam and Laurel. "This wasn't a shopper checking out the products. He followed me into the store this evening."

"He shoved you into the store, Logan." Sam looked at Aiden. "Then Miguel pushed him again. Logan got him to leave."

"You have two witnesses. If you want, I'll write an assault report and arrest him. The problem is, the judge will probably release him on his own recognizance pending a trial."

"It's not worth the hassle. My concern is for Laurel and Sam."

Aiden looked at Laurel. "When does the store open?"

She fought the urge to glare at him. "The day after tomorrow."

"You'll be working all day tomorrow?"

"Yes."

"All right. Keep your phone with you. Make sure my number is on speed dial. If Miguel shows up, call me. I'll do my best to drive by several times a day. You have employees, right?"

"Yes. All three of us will be working at the grand opening and the following day. Afterward, two of us will be working each day for the rest of the summer."

Aiden gave a slow nod. "Sam. Do you have a picture of Miguel? I want Laurel to show it to her employees."

She shook her head. "No. I threw them away when we divorced."

"I'll check to see if he has a drivers license. If so, I can get a copy with his picture."

They quieted when the waitress began setting down serving bowls filled to overflowing with fragrant Chinese foods. When finished, she left them alone. They ate for several minutes before Sam broke the silence.

"Do you have any idea who trashed the store?"

Aiden took a swallow of his tea. "No. We have a few cameras in Brilliance, and there's one next door showing the bank entrance, but nothing showing the front of Laurel's shop. We don't even know if it was more than one person. The alarm system installation wasn't completed, so the break-in wasn't reported until Laurel arrived the following morning. I'll add Hobson's name to the list of possibles. To be honest, we may never be able to identify the person responsible."

"I was lucky they didn't break the front windows," Laurel said. "What they did inside wasn't pretty, but not as destructive as it could've been. If they'd damaged the soda counter or display cases, the grand opening would've been delayed."

"All the floral arrangements were ruined," Sam said.

"True, but they could be duplicated," Laurel answered. "I did have to drive to Jackson for new containers, as the replacement order won't arrive until tomorrow. The biggest issue for me has been not knowing who did it and why they targeted my store."

Logan looked to Aiden. "Could it have been kids messing around?"

"I don't know. They knew enough to avoid the bank cameras or do anything that might identify them. My instincts tell me it's someone with an actual connection to Laurel."

She turned toward Aiden. "You mean you no longer believe I did it for the insurance money?"

Aiden grimaced, eyes clouded in pain. "I don't believe I ever accused you of that."

"Perhaps not, though you couldn't conceal your bias." Finishing her drink, she removed money from her purse and stood. "Thanks so much for helping me this afternoon, Sam. And for asking me to dinner. It was wonderful getting out of the shop for a while."

"You don't need to go alone. Walk back with us," Sam said.

"I'll be fine. See you soon." She waited until Aiden slid from the booth, moved past him, and left.

Aiden watched her leave until the door closed behind her. Letting out a sigh, he sat down.

"She's tired, Aiden. I'm sure she didn't mean anything by her comment."

"Sure, she did, Sam." Finishing the food on his plate, he pushed it away. "I should probably take off, too. Thanks for letting me join you."

"It was good to see you," Sam said. "Will you be at the grand opening?"

"I will. I've also asked Sheriff Duggan if he can spare another deputy. I doubt anything will happen. The same as the fires at Whistle Rock, whoever trashed her shop wants to stay anonymous. He's more likely to try again when the shop's closed."

Logan followed Sam back to Whistle Rock. He could've waved and gone on to his place. Instead, he parked beside her. Rounding his truck and hers, he stopped in front of Sam. Before she knew his intentions, he cupped her face in both hands, and staring into dark brown eyes, brushed a kiss across her lips.

He didn't hold her tight, giving Sam time to step away. To his surprise, she slid her arms around his neck to press her mouth against his. It lasted long enough for Logan to confirm how difficult it would be to continue pretending he felt nothing more than friendship for her.

Pulling away, he moved his hands to her shoulders as he took a step back. "I wanted to kiss you since spotting you at Laurel's."

"I'm glad you didn't wait any longer."

Chuckling, he ran a finger down her cheek. "Yeah. Me, too."

Sam glanced around, relaxing when she didn't spot any of the guests or ranch hands. "I should get inside before we catch someone's attention."

"I'll walk you to your cabin."

"No need. I'm capable of getting there by myself."

"I know. I'm still going with you. After all, you are my fiancée."

A slow smile broke across her face. "Not for real."

"Close enough." He took her hand in his, setting a slow pace across the expansive space between the large barn and lodge. Reaching the small porch, he kissed her once more.

"Thanks for dinner."

"You're welcome. Are you planning to help Laurel after work tomorrow?"

"I'll call to make sure she needs me."

"If she does, call me. I'd like to go with you."

"You don't trust Miguel to stay away?"

"That, and I want to spend more time with you."

She fell silent. He could almost see the wheels turning before she spoke. "What's going on, Logan?"

He shrugged. "I'm not sure. I just know being around you makes me feel good."

Studying his face, she nodded. "All right. I can accept that for now." Leaning up, she gave him a quick kiss before opening the cabin's door.

Sam opened the curtains of the front window, watching as Logan made his way back to his truck. She'd thought of inviting him in for coffee, knowing it would be a mistake. Their attraction to each other was too great to put them in a situation anyone on the ranch could misconstrue.

His comment about enjoying her company didn't surprise Sam. She felt the same about him. They'd spent a great deal of time together while packing and cleaning his mother's home. The more they talked, sharing their experiences, the greater her desire to spend more time with him.

The desire didn't erase the issues facing them. It also didn't stop the growing apprehension in her heart.

A spark of fear warning her anything so wonderful couldn't last.

Chapter Twenty-Two

Miguel Hobson strolled along the sidewalk at seven in the morning, stopping outside Brilliance Coffee & Bakery. He could see Lydia, the shop owner, through the front window. She sold the best coffee and pastries in town, often running out of popular items before mid-morning.

Twice, he'd tried to buy a glazed bar with maple icing but left with something else. Today shouldn't be a problem. It was early, and there were few customers inside.

The bell above the door jingled when he pulled it open, alerting Lydia of a customer. She glanced at him with a smile.

"Good morning, Miguel. How are you this morning?"

"Good, Lydia. Do you have any of your maple bars left?"

"I do. How about coffee with it?"

"Black. I'll add cream." He nodded toward the counter a few feet away offering sweeteners and several flavors of cream.

Paying, he found a table by the window. Before he could take a bite, Laurel Maddox appeared, heading straight for the counter. They'd never met, which was a pity, as she was a beautiful woman, and a widow. She was also a friend of his former wife, Sam.

Maybe he should ask Sam to introduce them. He smiled at the thought, knowing his ex would look at him as if he were nuts. Which he might be.

Laurel chose a table across the room against a wall. He watched her sip one of the frozen coffee drinks which had become popular over the last decade. Drawing several more sips through her straw, she opened the bag which contained what appeared to be a chocolate croissant.

Miguel watched as she took a large bite. Swallowing, her eyes lit up with satisfaction. He couldn't help smiling at the look of absolute peace on her face.

Lifting his cup, he took a sip. As he swallowed the hot, tasty brew, Miguel thought of how the length of time between satisfaction and dissatisfaction was often less than a second.

"Here you go, Logan." Laurel handed him a finished arrangement for placement on the top shelf of the refrigerated display case beside the front window. Topping off at seven feet, it was one of two oversized units she'd had custom built to match the original maple woodwork.

Two more custom units, shorter but wider, had been placed on either side of the soda fountain. The fountain eating counter had been refurbished with black granite. The sides were the original black and white marble. Twelve stainless steel stools had been cleaned and recovered with new black vinyl.

Sam worked with one of the employees to unpack, price, and display unique products for several existing cases. The registers, one for the floral counter, the other for the soda fountain, had been installed. Laurel and her employees had already spent time learning the system.

"There's someone pounding on the back door," Laurel said as she removed gloves. Several minutes passed before she returned. A delivery man pushing a moving dolly loaded with insulated boxes followed behind her.

"Ice cream and other food products for the soda fountain," Laurel called out as she moved behind the counter.

Sam's and Logan's eyes met, each smiling at her excited announcement. He closed the distance between them to rest an arm over her shoulders.

"What else can we do for you, Laurel?"

She turned toward them, brushed hair from her face before placing a hand on her hip. "Nothing more to do, Logan. You two have done much more than I expected. Thanks so much."

"We enjoyed it," Sam responded. "Wish we could be here in the morning. I'm sure your grand opening will be a great success."

"There will be lots of pictures for you to see. I'm going to make an album using one of those online services."

"You could keep it on a table for customers to look through."

"Great idea, Sam. I have the perfect table for it."

Logan looked out the window at the growing darkness. "If there's nothing else, Sam and I will head out."

The bell over the door jangled. Everyone turned to see Aiden, hat off, hair disheveled, take a couple steps inside and stop.

"You need to evacuate. There's a fire at the restaurant down the block."

Eyes wide, Laurel looked around the finished space. "I don't smell anything. Exactly where is it?"

"At the end of this block. Four buildings down in the new takeout place. Word is it's a kitchen fire. The fire department is already on it. You should be all right, but the sheriff wants everyone outside." He strode straight to Laurel, taking her arm. "You have to go."

Gritting her teeth, she shook off his hand. "I'm not leaving."

"Laurel, you have to leave. The odds are your shop will be fine, but you can't stay here."

Sam rushed to her. "Come on, Laurel. I'm sure it won't take long to put out the fire. You'll be back here in no time. Logan and I will stick around until we know everything is going to be all right."

"You don't—"

Sam held up a hand. "We'll stay. Right, Logan?"

"Absolutely. Let's go."

Logan couldn't shake the sense of being watched. Standing on the opposite sidewalk from Laurel's shop, he made a slow turn. He looked for one specific person, surprised when he didn't spot Miguel in the crowd.

The firefighters doused the blaze quick enough to save any damage to the buildings on either side. Brady Blackwolf had been in town with another ranch hand. As a volunteer firefighter, he'd jumped right in, helping as best he could. When they'd controlled the fire, he'd slipped out of his gear to join Logan, Sam, and Laurel.

"The fire doesn't make sense to me. It came from the back of the building. The captain didn't see a flashpoint in the kitchen, as he'd expected." Brady rubbed an arm across his forehead. "Best to leave all that to the investigator." He turned toward Logan. "I hear she's a real beauty."

"Who?"

"The new investigator."

Logan glanced at Sam, knowing she'd be listening. "Haven't met her."

"Me neither, but I'd like to."

Sam laughed. "You want to meet all the pretty ladies, Brady."

"I'll admit it's a serious flaw of mine. Time I got back to the ranch. Either of you need a ride?"

Logan shook his head. "No, we're good. We'll be staying a bit longer to make sure all is okay in Laurel's shop."

"Do you want me to stay?" Brady asked.

"Thanks, man. We're good. I'd appreciate it if you'd let me know what the investigator finds."

"Will do." Brady nodded at Sam and Laurel before taking off.

Logan kept his gaze on Brady until he lost sight of him. The same sense of being watched hit him. His head swiveled from one side to the other before he turned around.

"What is it, Logan?" Sam's expression turned from bland to concerned.

"I have an uneasy feeling someone is watching us."

Taking his hand in hers, she tugged to get his attention. "Laurel's ready to get back inside. Let's make sure she and her employees are all right, then drive back home." She stared up at him, her eyes imploring.

Releasing a slow breath, he nodded. "You're right. It's time to head back."

As he did the previous night, Logan walked Sam to her cabin. The kiss lasted longer, was sweeter and more intense than before. Each time he tried to drop his arms, they tightened instead. He didn't want to leave, but knew he couldn't stay. Breaking the kiss, he looked at her, noting her glassy eyes and swollen lips.

"I'll come down the hill to have dinner with you tomorrow."

"I'd like that."

He brushed another kiss across her lips. "Sleep well."

"You, too."

Walking to the truck, Logan's mind tightened as if in a vice. The same with his heart. Confusion clouded his thinking. The one thing he felt sure about was kissing Sam. There was no confusion regarding how much he liked it.

He'd come to loathe their agreement. A fake engagement didn't fit what he wanted from Sam. Not any longer.

Did he love her? Logan had no idea.

He'd loved his mother. The thought of her reminded him he'd never see her again. They'd never talk or spend another Christmas together. No one would ever fill the hole in his heart her death caused.

Logan wasn't as sure about his father or half-brother. He cared a great deal about Wallace and Quinn. The same with Abigail. But love? He didn't know.

Logan wanted to ask Sam how she felt about him. Uncertainty stopped him, unsure if he was ready for the answer. The way she melted into his kiss said something, but what?

The drive home took less than five minutes. He sat inside the truck for a long time, his mind still whirling around Sam and what, if anything, he should do.

The issue of Miguel continued to weigh on his mind. Could her ex be the arsonist? If so, what did he hope to gain by setting the fires? Could he have been the person who broke into Laurel's shop? What would destroying her store accomplish?

Nothing seemed to connect.

He kept coming back to the idea Miguel might not be involved in any of the actions under investigation. The fires might not be related, though the odds were slim. Did the break-in have anything to do with the fires?

Logan didn't envy Aiden his job. There were numerous possibilities, unanswered questions, and possible scenarios. As far as he knew, the deputy had uncovered few clues.

Aiden had accomplished something. He'd alienated Laurel, a woman Logan was certain the deputy had grown to care about.

Tired from a full day of ranch work, helping Laurel, sorting out his feelings for Sam, and trying to make sense of senseless actions, Logan released a tired breath.

He took a quick look out the front window of the truck toward his cabin. As with every other night, nothing alerted him to trouble.

Climbing out, he made his way to the front door of his cabin and disappeared inside, unaware of a lone figure scurrying into the shadows of Jake's house.

Chapter Twenty-Three

The grand opening of Laurel's Florals & Floats had been a huge success, drawing people from as far away as Jackson. Soda fountain customers consumed gallons of ice cream while floral arrangements flew out of the shop.

There'd been no incidents, such as the fire of the previous night. Maybe due to the number of deputies taking turns watching the shop, discouraging prospects from any malice. It didn't hurt to have Deputy Aiden Winters posted at the front door from six in the morning until nine at night.

Counting sales after the shop closed, Laurel couldn't help feeling elated. She knew there'd be more good days and lots of slow days. Even if average sales were a small fraction of what came in at the grand opening, her shop would be a success.

Several days later, Sam and Daisy arranged for a town tour with the new group of guests. One of their favorite stops had been Florals & Floats. There were so many positive comments, the Bonners made a town tour a regular activity for ranch guests. In return, Laurel and other shop owners provided special discounts.

There'd been no fires, break-ins, or cases of vandalism for weeks. Aiden Winters hadn't stopped by in almost a month.

The summer was giving way to fall, and the guest ranch was preparing for its last week of visitors. The last Sunday of the year when the staff would greet wide-eyed children and equally curious adults.

Logan and Sam spent most of their free time together, neither mentioning what should've been obvious to both. Logan hadn't admitted his feelings to Sam, and she'd been equally as quiet.

For the first time all summer, the two attended church together, sitting next to Daisy and Wyatt Bonner. They'd listened to a young, eager pastor deliver a message of hope and joy.

The words couldn't have come at a better time for Logan. It had taken a while, but he'd come to terms with his mother's sudden death.

As the service ended, Daisy leaned toward Sam. "Margie and Anson are taking care of Reece this morning. Why don't you two join us at Linda's Diner? She sets out a real good Sunday brunch."

"We'll meet you there," Logan whispered from where he sat on Sam's other side.

"Great. I'll let Wyatt know."

"I already heard you, sweetheart," Wyatt hissed under his breath.

Daisy rolled her eyes, sending a smile at Sam.

"This is excellent." Sam slid another bite of peach crepe into her mouth, humming in pleasure.

"All her food is great," Daisy said, cutting into her blueberry waffle. "Linda changes up the brunch menu every week."

"All I care about is her buttermilk pancakes and homemade maple syrup." Wyatt smiled as he spread butter on his stack of hotcakes. "How's your meal, Logan?"

"So far so good." He looked at his full plate. "I'm not sure what the soup is, but it tastes great."

"It's pozole," Daisy said. "She makes it with shredded pork and hominy."

The table grew silent as they ate. Sam spoke up when Logan and Wyatt left to refill their plates.

"Have you heard from Amanda Swanson?"

Daisy set down her empty cup of coffee. "I saw her at Lydia's last week. We were in line together. She hired someone to help with the ranch until it can be sold."

"She's selling?"

"She doesn't have a choice. Loans are coming due, and neither she nor Mark's parents have the money to pay." Daisy picked up a slice of bacon, taking a small bite. "She hired a man to help her work the ranch. Minimum wage plus board. The truth is, there are plenty of people who'd take that job and bank most of what they earned."

"How did Amanda sound?" Sam asked.

"All right. Not great. She doesn't know what she'll do once the ranch sells. I encouraged her to speak with Wyatt and Virgil. They may have some ideas."

"There must be someone in the area who could hire her."

Daisy nodded. "Probably. The problem is, she's expecting."

Sam's eyes grew wide. "Pregnant?"

"Yes. About four months along. She and Mark decided to keep it to themselves until she showed enough for people to notice."

Sam made a quick calculation. "The baby's due in February?"

"That's what the doctor told her. She learned last week it's a boy. Mark's parents want her to move in with them." Daisy looked up to see Wyatt and Logan returning to the table. "She wants to stay in Brilliance."

Sam understood. She planned to stay in the area as long as Whistle Rock Ranch offered her employment.

"What did we miss?" Wyatt sat back down, his plate loaded for a second time.

"I was telling her about Amanda Swanson," Daisy said.

Wyatt picked up his fork, then paused. "She's in a tough situation. Her husband died, the ranch is for sale, and she's pregnant. I expected her to call me or Virgil, but she hasn't."

"I heard Brady Blackwolf has gone to her ranch several times since Mark died to help her out." Sam set her empty plate aside.

"That's news to me," Wyatt said. "Virgil is probably aware of it."

Sam lifted her right shoulder in a shrug. "Word is, he's going on his own time. The same as his volunteer firefighter training. I'm going to call Amanda to see if she needs more help."

"If she does, I'm in," Logan said. He looked at Wyatt. "Have you considered buying her ranch?"

"It's a great location, the land is good, and there's plenty of water. Buying it would be splitting our operation to two locations. That wouldn't be efficient and would make it more difficult to run the guest ranch. I'd rather focus on a plan where Amanda could keep the ranch."

"Loan her the money?" Daisy asked.

"Pop will never go for it. As much as my mother likes Amanda, I doubt she'd support the idea, either." He stared down at his half-finished plate, inhaling a deep breath. Releasing it, Wyatt fell into an unusual silence.

Sam sat back, hands resting in her lap. "Whatever the answer, it won't be easy for anyone."

"Have you heard anything about Miguel?" Logan snagged Sam's hand as the two walked to her cabin.

"No. I wonder if he left Brillance."

Both knew what Miguel leaving the area meant. If he'd moved on, they were free to end the engagement.

"How would we find out?" Logan stopped on the porch of her cabin.

"I'm not sure. We could ask around. I wonder if he's still living in the room in town."

"I'll drive into town in the next few days and find out. I know where it is."

Sam's chuckle held little humor. "That's right. You followed him."

"Just the one time."

"If he's gone..." Sam's voice trailed off as her gaze once again settled on the guests.

Logan didn't need to hear the rest to know where her thoughts were going. Was he ready to end the engagement? What if he admitted his feelings for her? Did he want to take the risk she felt nothing for him?

He'd rather walk away as friends. Maybe the best path was to let their misadventure end.

"I should get inside. Tomorrow's going to be busy with the last group of guests for the season."

Relieved to move off the subject of Miguel, he nodded. "I have a long day tomorrow, too."

Leaning in, he kissed her. It was brief. Nothing close to how he wanted to kiss her.

"Goodnight, Logan."

"Have a good one, Sam."

He could feel Sam's eyes on him during the short trek to his truck. Logan wondered what was going through her mind.

They were at a precarious point in their relationship. He was, anyway. She might be more than ready to relinquish the fiancée title and return to being a friend. The thought of not seeing Sam almost every day felt wrong. Logan wanted the right to be with her whenever he wished.

First, he had to determine if Miguel had left town. And if he was gone? Logan would figure out what to do next.

Sam stared at the ceiling, switched to her right side, then her left, before counting cracks in the ceiling...again. She'd be surprised if she got three hours of sleep.

Brushing her short black hair, she tried to tame a stubborn cowlick with a touch of gel. "Darn thing," she muttered, twisting the lid back on the jar. Giving up, she grabbed a hat, shoving it over her head. Pushing her feet into a pair of well-worn boots, Sam lifted a lightweight jacket from a hook and headed outside.

Laughter from the corrals drew her attention. A group of twenty-somethings watched Barrel and Owen tack up their horses while telling stories of previous trail rides. Sam had heard the tales before. They never got old.

"Now, folks, this will be a short ride. Maybe an hour." Barrel slid the bit into his horse's mouth. "You might be thinking an hour is hardly worth the trouble. Believe me, if you haven't ridden in a while, you're going to be sore. I won't say where, 'cause I'm certain you can guess."

Sam laughed along with the others. In truth, Barrel was right. The guests getting ready to ride wouldn't be up for a second trip for two, maybe three days. For now, an air of excitement settled over everyone...except her.

Retrieving her horse, she tacked up within minutes and led the mare outside. She always loved getting to know the guests, where they were from, what activity most interested them.

Today, she asked the questions, even though none seemed important. Sam couldn't get her mind off Miguel.

It had been weeks since she'd seen him. Maybe he had left without bothering to let her know. She didn't care as long as he didn't create problems for her, Logan, or anyone else.

Chapter Twenty-Four

The group returned to the ranch two hours from when they'd started. The guests couldn't say enough about the lunch Beth and Abigail had packed for everyone or the scenery, including a beautiful waterfall.

Most opted to rest a while. The majority of women had signed up for Daisy's jewelry making class, while the men wanted to learn how to throw a rope.

The demographics were different than any of the previous weeks. No one was under eighteen. It didn't change the activities much, but did allow Gage to include one or two more challenging events.

Sam couldn't find it in herself to get too caught up in the activities for the final week. As always, she did whatever was needed to make the time special for the guests.

She had too much on her mind and no time to sort it all out. Miguel still hadn't appeared. Neither had Logan. No phone calls or texts. He hadn't stopped by or tried to set up something for the coming weekend.

Sam told herself it didn't matter. They were both busy. For whatever reason, the thought didn't soothe the strange ache in her chest.

"Silly," she murmured while storing the tack from another trail ride.

"What's silly?" Daisy stopped beside her, dressed as if she were going on a date.

"Wow. You look terrific."

"Thanks, and don't change the subject. What's silly?"

"Nothing, really."

"Must be something if you're talking to yourself."

Sam started walking toward the large double barn doors, Daisy right beside her. "I haven't heard from Logan in several days. We're both busy, so it seems silly to let it bug me."

"I can tell you it bothered me when Wyatt went several days without calling or texting."

"So, it doesn't seem odd to you?"

"Not at all. That doesn't mean you shouldn't wonder about it. Have you tried to contact Logan?"

Sam's brows drew together. "No. He's always the one to call me."

"Excuse me, but the world has evolved. It's okay for a woman to contact her fiancé."

"I know..."

"Maybe he's waiting to hear from you."

"You think so?"

"Hey, I'm no expert, but what would it hurt to call him? If you don't want to call, then text him."

"What if he doesn't respond?"

"Then you'll know there's something wrong. That's when you drive up the road and find him." Daisy checked her phone. "It's time to retrieve Reese from Grandma

Margie." She placed a hand on Sam's shoulder. "I'm sure it's nothing. As you said, he's as busy as you."

"Thanks, Daisy."

"Anytime." She waved as she jogged toward the main lodge.

Sam walked to the large corral used for demonstrations. Setting up another activity, she thought about Daisy's advice. She'd become complacent in the relationship with Logan. He always contacted her. Almost every day.

Taking a break, she walked toward the barn, tugging her phone from a pocket. Staring at it for several seconds, she wrote a brief text. Her thumb hovered over the send icon for another few seconds before she tapped it.

Logan heard the signal of a text had arrived. He ignored it, figuring the message came from one of the ranch hands or possibly his brother. Quinn knew he was knee deep in freeing a calf from a mudhole the animal had slidden into. He'd finish, clean up, and check the text.

The poor calf was scared to death. Logan didn't blame him. If he hadn't been out searching for strays, the calf could've drowned in the deep hole.

Almost half an hour passed before he tugged the little guy out and onto solid ground. His mother had never been more than a few yards away, watching and waiting.

Another hour sped by before he returned to the barn and washed up. Stomach growling, Logan warmed up some leftover lasagna Abigail brought over. Finishing every bite, he checked the time. He still had a couple hours of daylight left to finish a project in the barn.

It was almost seven o'clock before he thought to check his messages. Tugging out his phone, he opened his texts. There was one. From Sam.

His stomach clenched.

Logan had decided he needed some space. Not that she'd been crowding him. The opposite had been the case. It had been a hard and lonely five days since he'd seen her.

He'd learned to stay busy, pack his day from sunup to supper with work. No matter what he did, she'd never been far from his mind.

The text made him grin, and ache, at the same time.

How about pizza Saturday night?

The message made him miss her even more.

Over the last week, he'd learned Miguel had worked for Amanda at Kicking Horse Ranch. Logan's source, Brady Blackwolf, told him Miguel had left town two days ago, with a plan to head back to the Midwest. Logan didn't doubt it was true.

Miguel would never win Sam back. He could've stayed in Brilliance a hundred years and still not convince her to give him another chance.

Logan wondered if Sam knew of his departure. Miguel leaving could be the reason she wanted to see him Saturday night. With her ex gone, the need to continue their fake engagement could end.

If that's what she wanted.

For his part, he didn't want to let her go.

"Hey, Sam. You have mail." Owen held up an envelope.

She knew who sent it and smiled. Taking the envelope from Owen's outstretched hand, she stared at the handwriting and frowned. It wasn't her mother's distinct, flowing text, nor her father's small tight lettering. The return address had been omitted.

"Everything all right, Sam?"

"Um, yeah. It's all good. Thanks, Owen."

"Sure thing." He moved on, leaving her with a mystery to solve.

Opening the envelope, she unfolded the paper, letting her eyes slide to the bottom. A second later, she had her answer.

"Miguel?" Sam said the word as if it were a curse. She couldn't imagine what he had to say in a letter that couldn't be said over the phone, in a text, or in person.

Starting from the top, she read.

Samantha,

It took me a while to understand I should never have come to Brilliance. Your life is set. I'm still searching for mine. Anyway, by the time you get this, I'll be long gone. Not sure where I'm headed, but it'll be far from here. Tell your boss I'm sorry about the fires. Same for the damage to shop downtown. Just me blowing off steam. Have a good life, Sam.

Miguel

"It was him the entire time." She looked up, making sure no one was watching or had heard. Righteous anger had replaced curiosity.

Folding the letter, she slid it into the envelope before stuffing it into the back pocket of her Wranglers. Sam would have to let Wyatt and Laurel know what Miguel had done, as soon as the fury inside her faded.

It was Saturday morning and she still hadn't heard from Logan. She'd thought the invitation to meet for pizza would result in a response, but he'd never texted her back.

"Sam!"

Virgil strode to her. "We need your help with the last demonstration. Meet the others in the large corral."

"Will do. Is Wyatt around?"

"He's doing paperwork inside his office. Do you need to talk with him?"

Reaching into her pocket, she pulled out the letter, handing it to him. "I just received this."

Reading it, Virgil's jaw clamped tight. He scanned it again before handing the letter back to Sam. "Your ex confessed to everything."

"Yes."

"You need to get this to Wyatt right away. He'll want to contact the sheriff."

"I know. Maybe they'll be able to find him."

Virgil offered a slow nod. "Maybe."

Sam sat at a table with Brady and Jimmy French, listening to the band at Dulcy's. Her plans had changed when Logan didn't get back to her.

Maybe she should've talked to him in person. He'd want to know about Miguel, even if he had no desire to spend time with her.

"Here you are." The waitress set down burgers in front of each of them. "Anything else?"

"Not for me," Jimmy responded as she and Brady shook their heads. "I'm ready for this." He picked up the burger, taking a big bite.

Sam watched as Brady did the same. She'd been hungry when they'd ordered. All she could do now was stare at her plate. The aroma of the grilled burger caused her stomach to rebel.

"Not going to eat?" Brady asked.

"I'm going to wait a bit."

Sitting back, she looked around. The band was in the middle of a popular country song. Dancers crowded the floor. She could hear laughter from the bar, see smiles from customers at various tables. None of it affected her.

Between Miguel's letter and not hearing from Logan, she found it hard to enjoy herself. Driving back to the ranch to read a book, or head straight to bed, appealed to her more than the crowded, noisy saloon.

Then her gaze landed on a table across the room. Her throat constricted. Logan nursed a beer. Beside him, Laurel Maddox did the same.

Chapter Twenty-Five

Logan just wanted to be alone. He had a lot to think about, preferring to do it in the chaotic action at Dulcy's rather than the bleak silence of his cabin.

He felt bad about never responding to Sam. It was rude and unlike him to ignore her invitation. Something deep inside had him changing his mind each time he pulled out the phone.

Jake had come home with the news about Miguel, sharing it with Logan within minutes of exiting his truck. The information didn't come as much of a surprise. He'd known Miguel would do anything to capture Sam's attention. Hearing he'd set three fires and vandalized Laurel's shop was extreme. He hoped Miguel would be found, arrested, and brought back to face trial. Logan wished he could be on that jury.

The beer he stared at had been in front of him for a while before he felt a tap on his shoulder. Closing his eyes a brief moment, he hoped it wasn't a lovely lady wanting to dance. He would hate to turn her down.

Instead, he looked up to see Laurel Maddox. Shoving the chair back, he stood. "Good evening, Laurel."

"Hello, Logan. Mind if I sit with you for a bit?"

"Not at all." He pulled out a chair. "Are you here alone?"

"Just closed the store and wasn't ready to go home." Her chuckle held no humor. "Well, upstairs to my apartment, anyway."

"Are you meeting someone?"

"No. It's just me, which I don't usually do. What about you? Is Sam coming?"

"Uh...no."

The tone of his voice had her leaning in. "Trouble between you two?" When he didn't answer, she held up a hand. "Never mind. It's none of my business."

"Not a problem. It's complicated. My relationship with Sam, I mean."

"All relationships are complicated. It's just a matter of degrees."

Releasing a deep breath, he nodded. "We aren't really engaged."

"What?"

He nodded. "I'd appreciate it if you keep that to yourself."

"No problem. I am curious, though. Why would you agree to a fake engagement?"

Logan told her the story, ending with Miguel leaving town. "With him gone, there's no need to continue the deception." Taking a sip, he shoved away the glass of warm beer.

"How do you feel about Sam?"

"She's great. Perfect, in fact."

"I see. Does she know you love her?"

"I didn't say that."

"Logan, it's written all over your face. I've known for weeks, so most everyone else must've figured it out. Maybe even Sam."

He gave a quick shake of his head. "Nah. She's the type to say something."

"If you're certain you're in love with her, then you can't assume she doesn't feel the same. That's what you think, right?"

"Well, yeah. I mean, what do I have to offer her? My home is a tiny cabin at Jake's ranch. Don't misunderstand. I'm grateful for the job and cabin. It's just not suitable for a married man."

Her lips tipped up at the corners as she nodded. "I see. Well, my thought is she'd find your cabin more than suitable. That's assuming she loves you."

Letting his gaze wander to the dance floor, he pursed his lips. "She invited me to meet her for pizza tonight. I didn't respond to her text."

They sat for a few minutes in silence before Laurel spoke. "You know I'm a widow."

He nodded.

"We met at a saloon not much different from Dulcy's. A group of my friends would go there on Friday nights after work. Their drinks were priced right, the food good, and the crowd wasn't as rowdy as some places. Plus, they offered dance lessons. Line dancing and couples. One night, he came in with friends and he asked me to dance."

"Was he good?"

"Awful." She laughed. "He kept coming in on Fridays and kept asking me to dance until he finally invited me to dinner. But he was in the Navy, which made it complicated."

"Why was that?"

"His job entailed leaving the area without notice. One minute, his weekends were free, the next, he'd be on a plane. We managed to spend time together between those trips. I was all-in when he asked me to marry him."

"What happened?"

"We were married for over a year when he didn't return." She quieted, staring down into her lap. "Even knowing how our marriage would end, I wouldn't have changed anything. He was the love of my life, Logan. I was blessed with all the time we spent together. Don't miss the best thing in your life because you assume Sam doesn't feel the same."

She glanced across the room to a table with two men and a woman. "In fact, I'd recommend you tell her as soon as possible. Tonight would be a good time."

"Sam's not coming here tonight."

She nodded as her gaze moved to the other side of the room for a second time. "Are you sure?'

Shifting, he followed her gaze to see Sam staring right back at him.

Logan didn't remember standing, weaving his way between tables to stand next to her chair. "Hello, Sam." He lifted his chin at Brady and Jimmy.

"Logan."

"Having a good time?"

"Sure. You?"

"Not so much."

"Really? I saw you with Laurel. You must be enjoying yourself a little, anyway."

Logan's gaze moved from Brady, to Jimmy, settling on Sam. "Do you have a few minutes to talk?"

"You didn't return my text."

"I can explain. Just a few minutes, Sam."

"Go on, you two." Jimmy grinned. "We'll stay and watch the girls dance."

Rising, she followed Logan outside. She leaned against the building, arms crossed. "Okay. Explain."

Seconds ticked by in silence before he spoke. "It seemed so simple when Laurel encouraged me to talk to you."

"What does Laurel have to do with anything?"

"She's the one who said I should talk to you, let you know how I feel. It seemed simple...until now."

"Just say it, Logan. Then we can go back inside to our separate tables."

His nervous laugh was unexpected, though it did help relieve a little of the tension sparking between them.

"I heard about what Miguel did from Jake."

"That's what you wanted to talk about?"

"Well, no. It's just with Miguel gone, we need to talk about our engagement."

"The fake engagement, you mean?"

"It was fake at the start, Sam. Now," he released a heavy breath, "I'm not sure what it is."

"Over?"

"Not for me." Closing the distance between them, he tugged her arms apart, slipping his fingers through hers. Seeing the wariness in her eyes, he found the courage to continue.

"I love you, Sam."

She gasped, her eyes round with surprise.

"I don't know when it happened. All I know for certain is it did. Instead of ending the engagement, I want to marry you."

When she didn't respond, he went on. "I know I'm younger than you, don't have your experience in a relationship. I live in a tiny cabin, and don't know much about what the future holds. What I do know is I want you in—"

He couldn't continue with her arms wrapped tight enough around him to stop his speech. Enfolding her in his arms, he didn't think he needed to say much more.

They held each other in silence for a long time. He could feel her body tremble against his. Logan hoped it was a good sign. Edging away, he put a few inches between them.

"Is that a yes?"

Tears streamed down her face. He lifted a hand, sweeping them away with a finger.

"Darn. I never cry."

His eyes lit with warmth. "No?"

"Never. I don't know what's happening to me."

"But you'll marry me anyway?"

A slow smile appeared. "Yes, Logan. I'll marry you anyway."

He let out a loud whoop before capturing her mouth with his. Minutes passed before he raised his head to search her face.

"You're sure?"

She licked her lips, still feeling the tingle of his mouth on hers. "I love you, Logan. Marrying you is everything I want."

Epilogue

Two months later...

Sam held up her left hand to admire the gold band on her finger. Though she'd done it several times since the ceremony an hour earlier, she couldn't help doing it again.

She and Logan had hoped for a small, quick wedding at town hall. Once Margie and other women at Whistle Rock learned of their intentions, they put a stop to it real fast.

Being the sixth wedding at the ranch in the last few years, each knew their role and went to work. They worked with Sam, although she knew little about fancy wedding preparations.

Her parents had sold the ranch and moved to town. When told of her marrying a second time, they didn't wait to make flight plans. Sam was thrilled to see them, and they loved Logan.

"Sam, you are so beautiful. I'll bet the rest of the ranch hands wished they'd scooped you up first." Dorie Worrel, the local veterinarian, gave her a hug. "Men can be so blind."

"I won't argue with you, Doc. Are you seeing anyone?"

Dorie seemed surprised. "Not exactly."

"What does that mean?" Sam then saw Mack Devore, a local rancher, walking toward them. "Mack, huh?"

"He invited me to come with him. Nothing more."

"Right." Mack, a widower with two grown sons, had briefly dated Emma Griffin, a cook at the ranch. "He's a good man."

"That, he is." Dorie met him partway, sliding her arm through his.

"Guess you heard about the doc and Mack." Laurel stopped beside her, handing out a glass of punch. "Logan asked me to give this to you. Said he had to speak with Quinn about something."

"I don't know much about Dorie and Mack, except he invited her to accompany him today."

"They've been in Florals & Floats a few times together. I believe there's more to them than friendship." Laurel spotted Aiden Winters walking toward them. "I'm going to get a slice of cake."

Before Sam could respond, Laurel hurried off. She wondered if it had anything to do with the deputy, who appeared truly perplexed by Laurel's quick departure. He recovered to greet Sam.

"You look gorgeous, Sam." Leaning down, he kissed her cheek. "Congratulations."

"Hey, Winters. Are you messing with my wife?" Logan smiled at Aiden, clasping the hand held out to him.

"I couldn't help myself. She's the most beautiful woman on the ranch."

Slipping his arm around Sam's waist, Logan kissed her. "She is that. How are you, Deputy?"

"Good. Still hoping to find Miguel and arrest him. Other than him, Brilliance is a peaceful town." Aiden's attention shifted across the room, landing on Laurel.

"You should ask her out."

He looked over at Sam. "Who?"

"Laurel, of course."

Laughing, Aiden shook his head. "She doesn't want anything to do with me. Not since I had to ask questions about the fires here at the ranch."

"We heard about that," Logan said.

"I'll bet you did," Aiden replied. "I do like her. Sometimes, things don't work out as you'd like. Except right here with you and Sam. Have you decided where you're going to live?"

"For now, at my cabin. We'll figure it out from there."

A phone vibrating caught their attention. Aiden slipped his from a pocket. "Looks like I need to go. Let me know if there's anything I can do for you." He started to leave, then turned back. "I mean that."

Sam smiled at him. "Thanks, Aiden."

"He's a good man," Logan said.

"There seems to be an overabundance of them here today."

"What does that mean?"

"Nothing. Just a comment."

"I have some news, Sam."

She turned to face him. "Oh. What is it?"

Taking her hand, he drew her away from the reception crowd and into the large barn, then down the center between the stalls. When she started to open her mouth, he kissed her. After a while, he lifted his head.

"I love you, Mrs. Sawyer."

"I love you, too. Now, tell me. What news do you have?"

He pulled a card from the inside pocket of his coat, handing it out to Sam.

She scanned the card, her brows furrowing. "Who is this?"

"Never met him until today. He was in the area and stopped by. Had no idea there was a wedding taking place."

"Mr. Fred Salvato, Attorney at Law. Why would he be looking for you?"

"He said Mom hired him to take care of her affairs."

"What affairs?"

"That's what I asked him, Sam. Salvato told me Mom retained him to write her will and prepare a trust. He's been out of the country on vacation, not learning about Mom's death until he returned last week. Seems my mother had a few dollars with a financial firm. I always thought she lived paycheck to paycheck. The attorney said that wasn't the case." Logan shrugged. "Or maybe it was the case. She lived frugally and banked every extra dollar. She'd been doing it since her first job as a teenager working in a fast-food place."

"But she rented her small house and drove an old car," Sam said.

"She rented a house, but owned two apartment buildings in Cheyenne. Both are almost paid off. She lived off the rents, not her income at the law firm. Her paycheck was direct deposited into an investment account."

"Is there enough for us to buy a house?"

Laughing, he picked her up and swung her around. "More than enough, sweetheart. More than enough."

Learn about upcoming books in **The Cowboys of Whistle Rock Ranch** series at shirleendavies.com.

Enjoy the Whistle Rock cowboys? You might want to read **Macklins of Whiskey Bend**.

If you want to keep current on all my preorders, new releases, and other happenings, sign up for my newsletter at http://www.shirleendavies.com/contact-me.html

A Note from Shirleen

Thank you for reading **The Cowboy's Counterfeit Fiancée**!

Leave a Review! If you enjoyed the, please consider posting a short review and telling your friends. Word of mouth is an author's best friend and much appreciated.

I care about quality, so if you find something in error, please contact me via email at **shirleen@shirleendavies.com**

Books by Shirleen Davies

Contemporary Western Romance Series

MacLarens of Fire Mountain

Second Summer, Book One
Hard Landing, Book Two
One More Day, Book Three
All Your Nights, Book Four
Always Love You, Book Five
Hearts Don't Lie, Book Six
No Getting Over You, Book Seven
'Til the Sun Comes Up, Book Eight
Foolish Heart, Book Nine

Macklins of Whiskey Bend

Thorn, Book One
Del, Book Two
Boone, Book Three
Kell, Book Four
Zane, Book Five

Cowboys of Whistle Rock Ranch

The Cowboy's Road Home, Book One
The Cowboy's False Start, Book Two
The Cowboy's Second Chance Family, Book Three
The Cowboy's Final Ride, Book Four
The Cowboy's Surprise Reunion, Book Five

The Cowboy's Counterfeit Fiancée, Book Six
The Cowboy's Ultimate Challenge, Book Seven,
Coming Next in the Series!

Historical Western Romance Series
Redemption Mountain

Redemption's Edge, Book One
Wildfire Creek, Book Two
Sunrise Ridge, Book Three
Dixie Moon, Book Four
Survivor Pass, Book Five
Promise Trail, Book Six
Deep River, Book Seven
Courage Canyon, Book Eight
Forsaken Falls, Book Nine
Solitude Gorge, Book Ten
Rogue Rapids, Book Eleven
Angel Peak, Book Twelve
Restless Wind, Book Thirteen
Storm Summit, Book Fourteen
Mystery Mesa, Book Fifteen
Thunder Valley, Book Sixteen
A Very Splendor Christmas, Holiday Novella, Book
Seventeen
Paradise Point, Book Eighteen,
Silent Sunset, Book Nineteen
Rocky Basin, Book Twenty
Captive Dawn, Book Twenty-One
Whisper Lake, Another Very Splendor Christmas,
Book Twenty-Two

Mustang Meadow, Book Twenty-Three, Coming Next in the Series!

MacLarens of Fire Mountain

Tougher than the Rest, Book One
Faster than the Rest, Book Two
Harder than the Rest, Book Three
Stronger than the Rest, Book Four
Deadlier than the Rest, Book Five
Wilder than the Rest, Book Six

MacLarens of Boundary Mountain

Colin's Quest, Book One,
Brodie's Gamble, Book Two
Quinn's Honor, Book Three
Sam's Legacy, Book Four
Heather's Choice, Book Five
Nate's Destiny, Book Six
Blaine's Wager, Book Seven
Fletcher's Pride, Book Eight
Bay's Desire, Book Nine
Cam's Hope, Book Ten

Romantic Suspense

Eternal Brethren, Military Romantic Suspense

Steadfast, Book One
Shattered, Book Two
Haunted, Book Three

Untamed, Book Four
Devoted, Book Five
Faithful, Book Six
Exposed, Book Seven
Undaunted, Book Eight
Resolute, Book Nine
Unspoken, Book Ten
Defiant, Book Eleven

Peregrine Bay, Romantic Suspense

Reclaiming Love, Book One
Our Kind of Love, Book Two

**Find all of my books at: https://www.
shirleendavies.com/books.html**

About Shirleen

Shirleen Davies writes romance—historical and contemporary western romance, and romantic suspense. She grew up in Southern California, attended Oregon State University, and has degrees from San Diego State University and the University of Maryland. During the day she provides consulting services to small and mid-sized businesses. But her real passion is writing emotionally charged stories of flawed people who find redemption through love and acceptance. She now lives with her husband in a beautiful town in northern Arizona.

I love to hear from my readers!

Send me an email: shirleen@shirleendavies.com
Visit my Website: https://www.shirleendavies.com/
Sign up to be notified of New Releases: https://www.shirleendavies.com/contact/
Follow me on Amazon: http://www.amazon.com/author/shirleendavies
Follow me on BookBub: https://www.bookbub.com/authors/shirleen-davies

Other ways to connect with me:

Facebook Author Page: http://www.facebook.com/shirleendaviesauthor
Pinterest: http://pinterest.com/shirleendavies
Instagram: https://www.instagram.com/shirleendavies_author/
TikTok: shirleendavies_author
Twitter: www.twitter.com/shirleendavies